POINT OF NO RETURN

C.DASILVA

For my wife Marina,
The reason I live and love.

CHAPTER 1: NEW YORK 1884

Winter time brought two things to New York City — ice cold air, and death. As I looked down at my shoes covered in the snow of winter, I couldn't help but see the smoke flow out of my mouth with every breath. I hated winter with a passion but it was impossible for me to die because I was kept warm by the love of my beautiful wife, Evelyn.

We have been happily married for four years now, though we have the constant burden of not being able to conceive a child. I swear if Dr. Fitzgerald tells me my beloved Evelyn isn't pregnant next time, I'm going to take the glasses off his face and shove them straight up his ass.

There I go ranting again, of course I'm not. Poor Doc; it isn't his fault I'm cursed without a son to continue my bloodline. I was a single child and my parents died when I was just a boy, so if I do not conceive a child then my blood will come to an end. What am I saying? The curse will fade, I know it. Evelyn will get pregnant someday.

"Stop daydreaming my love," shouted Evelyn from across the road, waving her hand excitingly.

I have been waiting across the street for about fifteen minutes now. Evelyn works the night shift on Fridays down at Frank's Barber as a helping hand to keep his place tidy for the extra money. I hated that she worked there because of all the smug bastards that walked in there trying to win her over with money, but at the same time I couldn't complain. We needed the money desperately and I trusted her with my life.

"Hey, how was the shift?" I asked as I greeted her with open arms and a huge kiss.

"It was busy as usual— Christ, Lawrence can you not grow your beard like that?" Evelyn asked me as she cut herself off and pushed her face back scratching the itch that my beard had brought to her cheek.

I didn't say a word as a response. I just grinned childishly while rubbing my fingers through my full beard. She always reminded me daily that it looked like a bird's nest, but deep down inside I knew that she loved it.

Evelyn put her hands together and looked at me directly in the eyes. She seemed nervous. I couldn't put my finger on it but I knew she had something to tell me, and I was right. She cleared her throat and spoke.

"So I have something to tell you," she said. She grabbed my arm and pulled herself close to me.

"What is it?" I asked cautiously. I didn't know how to react to her. Should I be excited or nervous?

"Mr. Lawrence Talbot, you're going to be a father," she said with the biggest smile I had ever seen across her face.

"Christ! Really?" I asked. Of course there was no way in hell she would play with something that serious. I honestly couldn't say anything else to her since I was in shock and just wanted to scream for the whole world to hear just how amazing I felt inside.

I grabbed Evelyn with all my might and lifted her off the floor. Her dark hair fell onto my face but I could still see her beautiful chestnut colored eyes looking at me with utter beauty. She was gorgeous but I don't know what it is about the moonlight that always makes me fall in love with her all over again.

"I love you," I said as I pulled her in close.

"I love you too," she said as I pressed my lips against hers and kissed her with such joy.

"Will we be telling your family when we get there over dinner?" I asked as we began to walk down the street.

"I'm not sure, do you think we should, or maybe we should wait a little while longer?"

I understood Evelyn's fear in starting to tell everyone of her pregnancy. But I honestly had no family on my side and her parents were technically my only family. I wanted to celebrate with someone.

"I think we should keep it a secret to everyone outside of your family. I'm too excited to keep it bottled in so I think we tell them— but only them," I insisted

Evelyn looked at me and smiled calmly "if you feel that telling my parents is what we should do then we will tell them."

I gave her a quick, soft kiss as we continued down the street.

I'm going to be a father, I told myself as reassurance. If people knew me well enough they would definitely know Evelyn was pregnant just by the smile that was drawn all over my face.

We continued down the street for a few minutes without exchanging words to each other. I'm sure she felt the same way as I did, so excited with it all that the silence was just right to go along with our dancing souls.

"I was thinking if it is a boy, how about we call him Alexander?" I continued without letting her answer before I fully explained myself. "You know, named after my father."

"You know I really like your name, Lawrence, I would really like if our first boy carried your name as a junior"

I bowed my head low to the ground as I tried to think of a way of making us both happy. Then it hit me. "Wait, how about we incorporate both names together," I stated as I looked up at her.

"Alright what do you have in mind?" she asked intrigued.

"We can have my name, and also my father's name, maybe as the first.. like.. Alexander Lawrence Talbot Junior?" I said, stopping as I waited for her response. I could tell she was contemplating her version of the name.

"How about Lawrence Alexander Talbot Junior?"

"I like it," I said instantly. It had a real nice ring to it. Evelyn cracked a soft chuckle.

"What are you giggling at?" I asked as I gave her an outburst of laughter and a playful shove.

"You never mentioned a girl? What if it's a girl" she said flaunting herself to me. She obviously knew I had not even thought about.

"It's not a girl, so there's no point in even thinking about a name," I said sure of myself. I had a gut feeling my first child would always be a boy. A boy to take care of his younger siblings, being sisters or brothers— it didn't matter I was sure of it.

"How could you be so confident it's a boy"

"I don't know how to explain it to you but you have to trust me on it. If I'm wrong you can name her whatever you like and I will agree to it," I said grabbing her hand. "How does that sound?" I asked smiling.

"It's agreed then, Lawrence Alexander for our boy and whatever I want for the girl," she replied as she reached in. She looked at me with her beautiful eyes and I couldn't resist as we grabbed each other and kissed, never stopping as we continued down the street. We wanted to make sure we made it to her parents' house on time for dinner.

Knowing now that I was going to be a father, I felt the most carefree I have been in a long time. I had lost my job at the councilor's office as his assistant. Times were tough and the councilor couldn't afford my services, so I was let go. I owed one hundred thirty one dollars to a loan shark just so me and Evelyn wouldn't starve to death, and still I was two months behind on rent. God— one hundred thirty one dollars. That's like saying I practically had to starve two months, and honestly who could do that? When I was making sixteen dollars a week working at the councilors'. But for some odd reason I was carefree at this very moment, though the situation I was in could make any man stressed. It didn't make any sense but I wasn't going to ponder on it. I was just going to enjoy the company of the Baker's and worry about my problem later.

My in-laws lived just a few short blocks away in a crammed environment. It wasn't as bad as the poor immigrants that came to America to work had it, but it was definitely hard to live in such a little space. Why was I talking? At least my father in-law could afford his rent. John Baker worked down at the docks loading cargo six days a week for probably half of what I made. Though at one point I actually felt pity for him, and now I'm the one that's probably being judged.

"What are you pondering about?" Evelyn asked me.

I shot out of my deep thoughts as usual and looked at her. "It's nothing my love," I responded softly.

"Don't forget to ask my dad for that job down at the docks," Evelyn reminded me as I had already forgotten. Damn I really didn't want to work down there like a goddamn slave for pocket change. I had no choice. How else would I ever pay the loan shark off? That bastard has been harassing me for my money on one too many occasions. One time I thought things were going to get hairy when he appeared at my door with a knife. I begged him and he spared me a shiv— that was three weeks ago. I need money quickly. How long will I steer him off until he shivs me in the neck? Worst part of it all, Evelyn doesn't even know I got money from him. She thinks its money I got as a form of severance from the councilor. Sorry prick didn't even give me a nickel.

After some time we got to the Bakers residence. We walked up the stairs, I opened the door for Evelyn as she bowed a gesture of thanks and walked in, and I followed. The Bakers lived right on the first floor and it was the first door to the left. It was easy to remember because there were only four rooms on this floor. One on each side of the front of the hallway directly across from one another, and one on each side in the back.

Evelyn knocked on the door and we stood there for a moment waiting for someone to answer the door. We could hear someone coming and we prepared our smiles to greet the Bakers.

Instead, Conor opened the door. Why the hell was Evelyn's brother's friend here for dinner? I hated this loser.

Conor spoke in his stupid Irish accent. "Hey ya Eve, come on in," he said as he put his arm around her and walked her in. Me on the other hand I didn't exist. That's ok. I'll just walk myself in.

CHAPTER 2: THE BAKERS

As I made my way in, the first thing I noticed was that the fireplace that was fully stacked with firewood, as I could feel the warmth embracing every part of my body. Joseph, Evelyn's younger brother by a year, was coming out of the kitchen with a bottle of that new beer, 'Coors Light.' He approached me and I greeted him with a smile. I had met him a few times in the five years I had known Evelyn, but Joseph didn't come around very often. He was living down near the Five Points. The Five Points war had been over for a couple of decades but there were still plenty of gangs hanging around, trying to take leadership of the streets. Joseph was mixed in with some real serious shit. I'm surprised he was never found dead since all he does is hang out with his nationality of Irish folks. Rumors even had it that he was part of 'the Forty Thieves,' an Irish street gang that was founded in the eighteen twenties, and one of the oldest groups to still exist. Evelyn's grandfather was part of the 'Dead Rabbits' but he was killed with his gang and that was the end of them. Thankfully John never steered in his father or son's direction.

"Hey, ya Conor," Joseph called out as he walked by me and approached Conor and Evelyn.

"Yeh mate," Conor answered as he looked over at Joseph, by the way still with his arm around Evelyn.

"Get your greasy hands off my sister, and you watch it now, her husband is right there and will kick your teeth in if you don't stop touching her. Won't ya Lawrence?" Joseph asked me as he sat at the dinner table.

Conor got the picture and immediately took his arm off of Evelyn and cracked a grin towards me, completely mocking me as he slightly licked his bottom lip. Conor then made his way over and sat beside Joseph at the table.

I made my way to the kitchen, meeting Evelyn as we entered to greet her parents, John and Susan Baker.

Evelyn kissed her dad and then reached in and gave a big hug to her mother as she relieved the bowl of soup from her mother's hands and took it to the table.

I walked up to John "Hi pops, good evening," I said as I stuck my hand out to shake on it.

"Good evening Lawrence, how's the job hunting?" John asked as he firmly gripped my hand and welcomed me to his home.

"It's been tough to be honest. I actually need to talk to you about that," I said as I walked up to Susan and kissed her on the cheek.

"That's fine. We will continue this conversation at the table then," John said as he brought the cutlery to the table.

"Susan may I help you with anything?" I asked as I leaned against the kitchen counter.

"No, thank you Lawrence. I'm just making my way there myself," she said as she smiled politely and grabbed the plate of meat as she walked me out of the kitchen.

Everyone was already seated, as me and Susan made our way to the table. Joseph and John were at the heads of the table while Conor and I sat beside Joseph, and Susan and Evelyn sat beside John.

Susan got up and reached over grabbing the big spoon and pouring the soup for her husband. When Susan was done helping John and herself, Evelyn grabbed the spoon and filled her plate and mine.

"Hand the spoon over to Conor," Evelyn said as she passed me the spoon.

I passed the spoon over to Conor but Joseph reached in and snatched it out of my hands.

I shot him a confused stare as he returned a look to me and grinned.

"Conor can wait. I'm starving," Joseph said as he helped himself to the cabbage soup. Once he was done he gave the spoon over to Conor and the Irishman finally got to fill his bowl with what was left of the soup. Until now, Conor was actually being civil which was a big surprise. He always had a bone to pick with me and quite frankly I was getting tired of it.

"So Lawrence— what did you want to talk to me about work?" John asked as he slurped the soup from his spoon.

As I was going to explain myself of course, Conor stepped in. I knew it was too good to be true having a civil conversation with this douche bag around.

"You best not be asking for Papa John to be finding your lazy ass work," Conor said intensely.

John shot an angry gaze over at Conor. Joseph noticed his father's tension towards the interruption. "Shut your mouth Conor. Speak when you're spoken to," Joseph said calmly.

I could see the fear in Conors' eyes as he was motionless and then veered down towards his soup and continued to eat.

"I.." I had to clear my throat because of the elephant that was in the room which was making my mouth and throat dry. I couldn't find my voice. After a couple of coughs and some pushing of my throat, I found my voice.

"I was just going to ask if you knew if there was work down at the docks?"

"You have got to be shitting me? You going to let this slacker get a job down at the docks before me?" Conor interrupted angrily as he looked at Joseph for his opinion.

John smacked his hand angrily on the table. I could see Evelyn and Susan tense up and give a half jump clean off their seats. I was tense as I looked over at my father-in-law who had a bone chilling stare at Joseph.

John looked over at Conor and said "I'm trying to have a conversation with my son here. If you interrupt one more time I'm going to have to ask you to leave."

"Father that's not fair. Conor is right. You did promise him a job first," Joseph replied as he took a full spoon of soup into his mouth.

"How do you know I could even get Lawrence a job if I haven't even spoken yet?" John asked sarcastically as he was throwing those words toward Conor.

"You don't need to talk like that dad," Joseph answered now in an angry voice.

I could clearly see where this dinner was going.

Evelyn now stepped into the problem. " Alright guys, come now let's just have a normal dinner alright? We will just change the subject. So Joseph, how have you been?."

Joseph got up out of his chair angrily. "You know this is such bullshit," he screamed clearly very upset. "I'm never good enough"

John cut Joseph off. "Nobody is saying you're not good enough but you definitely have bad etiquette in how to treat your parents, when all you do is hang around with thugs," John stated as he pointed over to Conor.

Conor rose up out of his seat now fuming, "Hey mister don't you be calling me a thug when you got this Conniving thief over here trying to steal everything you got through your daughter's hand in marriage."

I was not going to take this son of a bitch's bullshit any longer. I got up out of my chair. Evelyn quickly rose up and held me back. I was ready to rip his head off.

"I'm not going to take this shit. You want to call him your son? Since you're having a conversation with your 'SON', then keep him. I don't need this shit anymore. Conor let's go. We're not welcome here. This unemployed beggar is more welcome than their own flesh and blood," Joseph stated as he walked by me and Evelyn, bumping his shoulder against mine making his way to the door.

"All because I asked for a job, this is ridiculous," I answered abruptly to Joseph who was grabbing his coat.

"This is more than just the job, Lawrence. This has been going on for far too long."

"How could you even know if anything is going on for too long when you're never around," I responded, so upset at this point that I wasn't even thinking about the consequences of what I was saying. This whole argument was unnecessary. If I didn't know any better, I would think this was all planned.

Conor came around the table and shoved me nearly into the fire as I hit my head against the fireplace.

Evelyn who was bumped aside when I was pushed, stumbled over her chair and fell to the ground.

John and Susan both sprang out of their seats and came between Conor and me now as I was getting back to my feet to attend to Evelyn.

Conor made his way to the door as he pulled out a knife from his pocket. Joseph already had the door open waiting for their exit as Conor said, " let me ever see your face again and I'll cut it clean off pretty boy."

"I want to see you try," I blurted out. At this point I was talking clearly out of my ass as I knew he wouldn't touch me since John was in the way.

Conor laughed aloud and looked over to Joseph who was just staring at me seriously. "You're all dead to me, and I don't need any of you," he said as he exited and Conor followed.

John went to the door and slammed the door angrily. He was tough as nails but I could see the fear and anger in his face as he came over to me to see if I was alright.

I was more worried about getting Evelyn comfortable on a chair. "Honey, are you alright?" I asked as I propped down on one knee and looked at her stomach.

"We're ok I assure you, but are you alright?" Evelyn asked me as she reached in and moved my long hair aside to see my forehead.

"Yes, this is nothing. It's just a bump," I answered as I got back up and kissed her hand.

Susan was now hugging John and crying into his shoulder. Clearly, having a son disown his family was hard on any mother and father. I hoped my son growing inside Evelyn would never disown me. Hell I would kill him myself if he ever thought he could get away from his father. I never had a father and so I wanted to make sure I was there for my children every moment I could.

"Mom, Dad? Me and Lawrence have something to tell you," Evelyn said as she got up and nervously grabbed my hand, looking at me to say the news.

I looked back at Evelyn with a joyous smile and then we looked at John and Susan and I announced "Me and Evelyn are expecting our first child."

The sorrow in John and Susan's eyes vanished as they quickly became filled with joy. They then practically hugged us to death.

"Oh God bless you both," Susan said as she kissed us.

"I hope he has my looks," John said as we all laughed. He hugged me the hardest he ever had, I think the only time he hugged me with that much emotion was the day I married his daughter.

"Come now, let's go and celebrate," John said as he reached over the fireplace and grabbed two cigars out of a wooden box. He handed me one and walked over to the door. We quickly put our coats on and we went outside to the front steps. I put the cigar against my lips and slightly pulled in while he lit the tip for me. I could feel the slight tingle at the tip of my tongue since I probably had smoked two cigars my entire life. I pulled in hard and then released the smoke as I choked. John laughed out loud, deep from his gut as he lit his cigar up.

"You know I can put you down at the docks. I wanted to tell you but Susan mentioned that maybe it would be degrading for you so I didn't mention it," John explained as he pulled on his cigar and twisted his mouth to blow the smoke up towards the night sky.

"John, no not at all. I wish I had known"

"The pay is not bad. It's a buck a day, six days a week" John explained as he took another pull from his cigar.

He clearly smoked more often than I did as I was trying to let mine mostly burn so I wouldn't have to choke to death or embarrass myself in front of him.

"I never put Conor in because I don't want those thugs working down at the docks with good hardworking folks. They're criminals and that's what they are— even Joseph. They're just criminals so they will cause trouble anywhere they go. But you— you're a good kid and I will find you work."

"Thanks John, I really appreciate this," I said as I took a pull on the cigar. But this time, I didn't almost cough a lung right out of my throat.

"Are you free tomorrow?" John asked as he tapped the end of the cigar with his index finger to drop the burnt ashes off the edge.

"Yes, of course, anytime," I responded quickly to show John my seriousness of this job.

"Alright, come down to the docks tomorrow at let's say— ten o'clock and I'll get you to speak with my supervisor. He will hire you for sure," John said with great confidence. "I'll put in a good word for you," he added as he winked.

I smiled and took in another pull of the wretched cigar that was literally making my tongue go numb.

"You know, Joseph wasn't always a troublemaker. He was a good kid. But when we settled here in the late sixties, we were poor and lived down at the Five Points. That was where we lost him forever. I settled there because I grew up in the area so I was familiar with it. He grew up around the poor life and began thieving and getting into trouble with the law early on," John explained to me. This was new to me as I honestly didn't know anything about Joseph, just his name and that he was a thug that lived down at the Five Points.

After about ten minutes when John had finished his cigar, as he was looking up at the sky, I killed my bud against the wall and put the rest of mine in my jacket to pretend I had finished and we went back inside.

The warmth against my frozen cheeks caused a prickling pain that hurt but also felt very good at the same time. I rubbed my hands together to cause a friction and blew into them my hot breath. "Honey, you ready to go home?" I asked as I continued to heat up my hands.

"Yes, I just finished the table with mom," Evelyn said as she came to the door to grab her coat that was laid out on a chair.

John took off his coat and rested it on the back of his chair and came to the door with Susan to say there good byes.

"Alright, thank you for having us," I said as I hugged Susan and shook John's hand.

"You have brought us warmth into our hearts," Susan responded as she cried tears of happiness.

Evelyn hugged and kissed her parents and we were off towards home.

CHAPTER 3: SETUP

As we made it to the front door of our apartment complex, I glanced at Evelyn and threw her a smile as I reached into my coat and grabbed the keys. Suddenly a few yards out there was a huge crashing sound as a nearby shop's window was shattered into a million pieces.

I opened the door to the complex.

"Sweetheart, get inside. I'm going to see if Mr. Finagin is alright."

"Wait just let the cops deal with it," Evelyn responded as she clearly feared for my safety.

"I'm sure it's nothing honey. I'll be right back," I said as I kissed her on the cheek and made my way down the street in a hurry.

"Be careful," Evelyn shouted as she closed the door behind her.

I ran straight to the accident and could hear two people arguing inside the shop. I stopped just outside the sidewalk. I was trying to make out who was inside as there were no candles lit up. After a brief moment, I summoned the courage to call out "who's there? Tom is that you?" I asked but there was no response.

I stepped in just at the point where the window met the sidewalk and from the shadows came a pistol, as it pressed itself right to my temple.

"Get inside," ordered a man with a foreign accent.

I didn't put up a fight as I was just thinking about getting back to my family. I walked right in and was led to the basement where Mr. Tom Finagin was tied to a chair.

"Tom are you alright? What's happening here?" I asked but Tom didn't respond as he was struck with fear.

The man pressed the pistol against my back and shoved me closer to Tom. He then walked back and stood at the top of the steps almost like he was waiting for something or someone. After a few moments, I could hear a chariot approaching. The culprit rushed down the stairs and didn't say a word. He just raised his pistol and shot Mr. Finagin. Tom fell back off the chair right by my feet. The culprit, for some odd reason, tossed the pistol at my feet and ran upstairs in a hurry.

I couldn't believe what I was witnessing right in front of me. I had never seen anyone get shot before. I got down on one knee right into the pool of blood and checked for a pulse. Tom was dead. I sat there for a moment contemplating my next move. I began to feel the panic setting in and I ran to the corner as I began to hyperventilate. I couldn't hold the supper I had with Evelyn and her family, as my stomach was beginning to tighten and turn upside down. I threw up all over the floor.

"Sir are you alright?" came a voice just above me, as I looked over, wiping the vomit from my beard. I noticed it was cops.

"What happened here?" one of the officers asked me as his partner went over to the deceased man and knelt to examine him.

"Looks like this man was shot sir," the crouched officer said to the officer now approaching me.

"Being that you're the only person at this crime scene makes you the prime suspect than" the cop said as he took out his cuffs. It was a bad system. The cops were more corrupted than most and they definitely didn't want to have to work, so they would just take me without question.

"Sir, please I was just entering my home when I heard the window shatter. I came here to see if Tom was alright and when I got near I heard an argument. I was led down here at gun point and then a man shot him," I said as I pointed towards Tom's body.

"You mean with this gun here?" asked the officer rhetorically near the deceased man, as he held the gun up with his thumb and pointer finger.

I was clearly set up. Someone had actually planned to get me imprisoned.

"Save that for your statement down at the station," the officer near me directed.

"I beg you, my wife is pregnant and I need to get to her. I have been set up."

"For your sake you, better hope you're innocent or that child will not have a father," the officer said as he swung me around and cuffed me.

The officers escorted me to their chariot and led me inside, slamming the door behind me. As they got in the chariot and began to ride into the night, I watched my home drift away as we turned into another street.

Who the hell would honestly want to set me up? This clearly didn't make any sense. It must be a coincidence. It couldn't be. That man was waiting for the police to arrive to shoot Tom. This is such bullshit.

Coming from the other direction were two police chariots heading to the crime scene. My chariot came to a sudden halt. I could hear one of the officers informing the others, "I got a suspect. Just contain the scene until the coroner arrives."

As fast as the chariot had stopped it now began to move again.

What of my child's future without a father if I didn't make it out of this a free man? As I pondered deeply into my ever working mind on possible scenarios that were about to happen to me, the chariot came to a complete stop. After the approaching footsteps came to my door, it swung open. The officers grabbed me and practically dragged me inside their main headquarters on Mulberry Street.

All the officers inside stared at me as if I was practically guilty already. I kept my head down and tried to avoid eye contact as they brought me into a small room which only had a table and two chairs. They sat me down and released my cuffs. I rubbed my wrists as they burned from the steel against my skin.

"Put your arms behind the chair," demanded one of the officers.

"I assure you this isn't necessary," I responded but I swear those officers were already treating me like the culprit. The officer quickly grabbed my arms pulling them back, almost popping my shoulders straight out of their sockets and cuffed my hands to the chairs back.

"Please I beg you, I'm innocent!"

The now exiting officers kept walking, completely ignoring me. They shut the door behind them, leaving me in that empty room with only me and my thoughts.

I sat in there for at least ten minutes just waiting for someone to come in but nobody entered. The nerves I was experiencing at the thought of getting locked up while innocent and not being able to see Evelyn had me feeling like I was going to yack again. As I let my head hang loosely from my neck, stretching every muscle straight to my tightened shoulders, the door opened.

In came an older man with years on his face for sure. The white combed hair and pepper beard were a dead giveaway.

He calmly grabbed the backrest of the chair across from me and slid it back, allowing himself space to take a seat.

"I'm Detective Owen Murphy and I have been assigned to this case," he said firmly as he stared into my eyes.

"Sir I assur—"

The detective just held his index finger over his lips, addressing me to silence myself.

"Everyone is innocent until they're proven guilty and I'm not saying you are, but let's just get your story down so that we can decide what to do, alright? If this was twenty years ago, you would be hanged in the morning without question but now we got a new process and people have rights. So let's do this," the detective explained as he sat there calmly examining me.

"Alright, what do you need from me?" I asked, as I took a big gulp.

"I simply need your honesty," the detective said, as he took a paper, a little jar of ink, and his pen out from his jacket and placed them on the table. The detective then got up and came behind me, unlocking my chains. "You try anything and you lose all your rights. I can trust you right?" he asked as he reached in close to my face from behind me.

I awkwardly looked at him since he was so close. "Yes you can trust me," I replied.

The detective took a whiff of my breath. Wow he's clever. He actually wanted to see if I was drunk.

"Cigars, nice I like cigars," the detective said as he walked back around the table and sat back down on his chair. The detective then grabbed the pen to begin writing.

"Alright, start from where you were prior to the scene of the accident," Detective Murphy said.

"I was waiting for about fifteen minutes for my wife, Evelyn to get off work."

"Where does your wife, Evelyn work?"

"She works down at Frank's Barber on Thirty-First and Main."

"How many days a week does she work there?" the detective quickly shot, as he adjusted his posture.

"She works there only on Fridays Sir." I took a big gulp before continuing; "Only night shifts."

The detective nodded as he wrote the information down on his paper.

There was a moment of awkward silence as he wrote. He then dipped his pen into the ink and continued writing some more.

I hope to Christ this man believes me.

The detective took a deep breath and took off his jacket, placing it neatly on the back rest of his chair.

"I'm told your wife is pregnant," Detective Murphy asked. I didn't have the slightest clue as to what that would have to do with a murder investigation. How could he even know she was pregnant. I don't recall ever telling anyone, wait— I did tell the officers at Tom's to avoid being arrested.

"Yes she is I just found out a few hours before the accident."

"Well congratulations to you and your wife. Now, she gets off work and then what happens?" Detective Murphy asked as he dipped his pen into the ink jar and prepared to continue writing.

"We walked to my in-laws and stayed there for a few hours, as we had supper and then we came home."

"When did the accident happen? Where was your wife?"

"We had just arrived at the front of our home on Fourth Street. I was just about to unlock my door when we heard the crash."

"So what, you opened the door and told Evelyn to stay inside while you played hero?" I swear the detectives tone was becoming almost sarcastic. This was probably one of his tactics to get people nervous to slip if they were guilty. But I'm not guilty so I won't get nervous, his tricks won't work on me.

"That is exactly what happened. Well I wasn't playing hero but I wasn't going to go inside like nothing happened."

"Alright so you tell your wife to go inside and then what?"

I flinched my eyebrows now at the detective since obviously I ran to the scene.

"It's just protocol to know how one gets from point A to point B. Just answer the question," the Detective insisted.

"I ran down the street as fast as I could and when I got to the scene I heard someone arguing."

"You were there when the man was shot?"

"Yes, I was held hostage at gunpoint and led downstairs beside Tom."

The detective didn't look at me as I told him that. He just continued to input his information on his paper.

"You can look in the corner of the basement. Would a murderer throw up at his own crime scene?" Why the hell did I just say that? Now he was definitely going to think I was trying to veer off the conversation, when really all I wanted was for them to find my vomit. That had to prove I was innocent, at least I hoped.

"So you couldn't hold your supper in once you saw all that blood?"

"It was gruesome. I have never seen that much blood in my life. When the culprit shot him, Tom died instantly."

"Tom Finagin. His name is Tom Finagin"

"Alright Tom Finagin was on the ground dead in a pool of his own blood."

"Yes, blood that came from a gunshot to his neck. His wound was very fresh like it had just happened a few seconds before the cops arrived. They verified that because they heard the shot go off," Detective Murphy said as he chuckled and then began to cough harshly into his sleeve. He seemed excited. I think he was convinced I was the culprit. After getting himself together again, he veered a deep gaze towards me that sent a chill down my spine.

"Tell me why did you kill..."

A knock came from the door and it opened, revealing a female with ginger hair.

"Owen, we have eye witnesses that say they saw this man making his way down the street, and that means the glass had already been shattered"

Detective Murphy threw his gaze upon the female as he rose to his feet abruptly, "Annie you're telling me someone shot Tom and fled without us seeing him? There is only one exit which was clearly the way the cops came in from?" the detective burst out as he pointed at me with bad intention.

Annie just nodded towards Owen in agreement to his statement.

Owen quickly looked over at me and nearly propped himself over the table. "I know it was you, we'll keep in touch," he said as he looked away clearly upset.

I rose off my chair in a hurry. "Excuse me detectives," I said as I made my way out the door. I then turned back and propped my head back into the room, being the shit disturber I am." I do truly hope you find the killer." As I quickly propped my head back into the hallway, I got a quick glimpse of Detective Murphy's angry face. I then quickly rushed down the hall. I didn't blame the guy. If he didn't find a culprit, he didn't get paid. But still I was innocent and thanks to Annie for saving me I got to see my family again, I owed her one.

As I opened the doors of the station, I rushed down the steps and literally had to lean against a lamp post to gather my wits at how that was 'too close for comfort.' As I collected myself, I noticed how much I was covered in blood from the waist down. The smell of puke in my breath was almost unbearable and I was surprised the detective didn't faint during our interview.

A silent chill passed and sent a sudden shiver through my entire body. The stinging feeling in my hands and face reminded me of how cold it still was outside and that helped me find the strength to quickly get home.

CHAPTER 4: POINT OF NO RETURN

What seemed like forever to walk home finally came to an end when I stood in front of my house steps. I was absolutely frozen and my feet were throbbing with a deep pain almost in the form of a heartbeat. There was such an intense pressure, especially on my big toes that I was afraid to take off my boots and see that my nails had popped clean off.

I looked down the street at the site of the crash while reaching for the key in my pocket. I tried my hardest to focus as my eyes were beginning to blur from exhaustion of being up late into the night. I put the key in the door. I could see officers stationed at the scene and a handful of civilians hanging around. I then pushed the door open as I pressed into it still with the key inserted. It was peculiar since Evelyn and I were always very careful about keeping the door locked to avoid theft. The door was left unlocked. As I walked through the door, I shouted "Evelyn!" but there was no response. My heart began to pound inside of my chest. I was probably overreacting but of course I was such an anxious wreck all the time and I feared the worst with every situation.

"Evelyn." I shouted again but still no answer. I quickly took off my wet worn out boots and climbed the few steps into my hallway. The hallway candles were off but there was a dim light creeping in from the living room and so I made my way. I walked to the door of the living area and turned the corner. There sat Vlad Reznik, my goddamn loan shark!.

He sat there with a grim look on his face as he held his knife tightly around Evelyn's throat.

"Do you know how many times I have asked your pathetic husband for my money?" Vlad asked Evelyn. His face was dangerously close to hers. He licked her cheek with his tongue, which sent me into a hellish rage. I knew the bastard was doing that to get a spark out of me and damn did he know how to make it so. I charged at him with clenched fists as I was ready to break his face but I was tackled by two men who appeared from the kitchen. I didn't have much furniture but I definitely had one less piece now. I lay flat out on what was, just a moment ago, my dinner table. This monstrous Russian man laid over me holding me down. The second man wasn't lying on me but he was perched over making sure his hand was fluttering my face to distraught my breathing and focus.

"Get that fool back on his feet," Vlad ordered and the two men got me back up quickly as they punched and kicked me in the sternum to calm me down. I could feel my organs tightening with each blow but I was so focused on my wife and child's safety that I kept my eyes on Evelyn.

She was terrified but kept her eyes on me also.

"What's going on Lawrence? Who are these people?" Evelyn shouted at me confused.

"I wanted to tell you, Evelyn. I did. I never got a severance pay from the councilor."

"What?"

"I didn't want to worry you, so I got the money any way I could."

"The money you brought home was this man's money, not the councilors?"

"That's exactly what I'm saying," I said as I bowed in shame.

"That's not a problem at all," Evelyn assured Vlad as she looked over with a composed smile. I could see her fear through her fake smile. Problem was that she didn't know Vlad like I did. He had waited a long time and he didn't want to wait anymore. "Look there in my jacket. I got four dollars I made tonight. Grab it and we will bring you the rest tomorrow," she assured.

Vlad grinned as he let Evelyn go and reached for her jacket and grabbed the money observing the coins. He slipped the coins into his jacket pocket and walked over to me. I tensed up as I had my eyes fixated on his knife.

"Now you owe me one hundred twenty seven dollars, but I want it now."

"Wait, how much?" Evelyn asked in shock.

She knew about sixty dollars but not this much. I was definitely in trouble.

Vlad looked over at her. "Did I stutter my words, woman?" He asked rhetorically as he walked over to her. "Now listen, bitch. Thanks for the four bucks but I need you to stay quiet for a while and let the boys have their long overdue conversation alright?"

Evelyn went red to the face. "How dare you call me names in my own home."

Vlad released a quick smack across Evelyn's face that sent her crashing to the ground.

"Don't touch her you son of a bitch. I swear I'll kill you!" I belted as I tried with all my might to get loose of the two that held me.

Vlad walked over to me and gave me a cold stare. "Sorry, what did you say? I couldn't hear you." As he finished his words, he punched me in the face, hard. I was in a sudden daze as my neck got serious whiplash as it shot back hard. He cuffed my neck with his hand and drew me close while whispering in my ear softly. "Last chance you shit. Where's my —money?"

I blinked once heavily to catch my focus, as my eyes were blurred. Everything was taking its toll on my body all at once— no sleep, the interrogation, the murder I saw, and now seeing my family in danger. Honestly, I couldn't care about me as long as my family was in danger.

"Alright that's enough. Just hold him there," Vlad said as he turned his back on me and approached Evelyn. She was sitting on the ground and propped up holding her cheek and swollen lip. The two orcs that held my scrawny build, which was no more than a tree twig to them, held me firmly as I continued to try to shake my way free.

The closer Vlad approached her the more I lost my voice in panic. I finally found some words. "I swear to you I will have it for you tomorrow."

"NO! I want my money now!" Vlad roared as he grabbed Evelyn by the hair and pulled her up to his side.

"Please, Vlad don't hurt her. Please just wait until tomorrow and I swear I'll get it all for you."

"That sounds promising. Ok I'll make you a deal," Vlad said as he shoved Evelyn onto a chair that was next to him. His voice carried sarcasm and I knew he was up to something. "I'll kill your wife and I'll spare you. But if you don't bring me my money, I'll kill you too."

"NO! Please don't hurt her."

"Please don't hurt me. I'm pregnant," Evelyn announced in an effort I was sure she was hoping to find some sympathy in his heart.

"Don't blame me honey. Your husband killed you and your child, not me," Vlad said as he pushed Evelyn off her chair and she crashed to the ground.

"VLAD! I told you I will get you the money. Please don't hurt my family." At this point I was literally crying aloud and if I could get free and fall to the ground I would beg on my knees and kiss this man's boots.

Vlad laughed aloud and so did his goons. They definitely didn't care about anything I was saying. They had definitely come here with their minds made up already. I could see it in their faces and I realized there was no way out of this. I tried to fight off the two men but their strength held me back. One of them punched me across the face and I was severely dazed again.

"You don't scare me at all small man, and I WANT MY MONEY!" Vlad belted as he grabbed Evelyn and stabbed her multiple times in the chest. My beloved Evelyn tried to hold him back but her strength faded with each stab. Her fainting eyes veered over towards me as her face slipped off her buckling shoulders.

My world was shattered before my eyes. My eyes were blurry but I had seen just enough to know I had lost everything.

All I saw was red. I tried to break free so that I could squeeze the life out of Vlad with my bare hands but one of the goons pulled out a baton and cracked me in the skull. I hit the ground hard.

Vlad crouched down towards me. I couldn't see him since I was stunned but I could smell his sweat and I knew it was him from previous encounters. "I want my money tomorrow. Sorry for your loss," he said as he and his goons giggled and left the apartment.

I crawled towards Evelyn as fast as I could, which wasn't fast at all. I could hear her weeping and her breathe becoming faint. "I'm sorry, Evelyn" I tried to free my words that were being cut by my sobbing. "I wasn't strong enough to protect you. I'm so sorry, my beloved," I said as I tried to comfort her in her last moments. I ran my fingers through her blood stained hair and kissed her forehead. My tears dropped quickly on her face while I lay her head on my lap. As I sat up, I had one hand on her cheek and the other was being wiped across my face to stop the tears.

"...d...d...," Evelyn tried to speak but her faint breathing was interfering with her speech.

"Save your strength, Evelyn."

"..don't...blame..your...self." With those simple words my beloved Evelyn was gone from this world forever.

"EVELYN! EVELYN! NOOO! NOOOO!" I roared.

I could hear approaching footsteps and for a brief moment I thought that maybe Vlad had a change of heart and was just going to execute me also. I was wrong. I looked up towards the entrance door and saw two police officers staring at me, shocked while grabbing their batons. Someone must have heard the disturbance and called the cops.

"Sir, calm down and step away from the woman," the officer closest to me ordered firmly as he stuck out his palm.

I managed to talk through my sobbing, "My wife was murdered just a moment ago. We owed money and they got aggressive, and now my beloved is gone." I held her lying dead corpse as close as I could as I sobbed uncontrollably. What was the point in living now that I had lost her? Then it hit me. I could feel a fire burning deep inside. The feeling one gets when they want.. Retribution.

The officers moved another step closer towards me, still holding their batons, waiting for an excuse to use it on me. I had just come from the station and Detective Murphy already thought I had killed Tom. There was no way in hell I was walking away from this, not that I cared. I didn't care for my freedom because without Evelyn I didn't want to live anyway. But I couldn't die until I killed those who had taken her life.

I slowly placed Evelyn's dead corpse on the ground. I closed her eyes with my finger tips and gave her a gentle kiss on the lips. "Evelyn, I love you with all my heart and I will avenge your death. I promise no matter the cost."

"SIR, STEP AWAY FROM THE WOMAN!" the officer now shouted as the two officers prepared to take me into custody by force.

As I got up on my feet, I cleaned the tears from my face. I felt nothing, just an empty shell.

"I'm going to check her pulse. Step back," the officer in the back demanded.

I wanted a miracle to happen and so I stepped back a couple of steps until my back heel touched the wall. The only thought that came to my mind was that Evelyn would open her eyes and this would all have never happened, like a bad dream.

The officer made his way over to Evelyn and checked her pulse. He looked over at his partner and nodded to him hinting that she was indeed dead. As the cop rose to his feet they both looked at me, ready to strike.

No matter the cost, I would avenge her death and nobody in this world could stop me. I knew I had only moments to react and so I did. I ran as fast as I could at the cop that had just got to his feet and shoved him back down to the ground. I then ran towards my kitchen.

The second cop tried to grab me but I shook free. My jacket sleeve ripped but I still managed to get away from his grasp. I leaped out the tiny window that was right above the kitchen sink. Evelyn always called the little window, "The Creeper".

A six foot drop feels like one hundred feet when you put your all into a jump. I felt like I broke every rib in my body, but I managed to get back up quickly.

"Go get the others!" the cop in the kitchen shouted as he also leaped out the window.

I didn't look back. I began to run as quickly as I could down the dark alley.

CHAPTER 5: ON THE RUN

I began to run through the slums weaving around and over garbage. Clothes drying on the hanging lines also became an avoidance as it was easy to get tangled in the them. The persistent cop who was just trying to do his job was really beginning to worry me. "I need to get away" I kept repeating to myself. At this point my exhaustion was so intense that I was using my revenge as the coal in my tank to keep pushing forward.

The frozen air that was rushing by my ears and hitting my body as I ran didn't help my escape. The pain that it was causing my skin created more of an obstacle then any turn or hanging line I had to avoid. I could feel myself slowing down. As I looked back over my shoulder, I could see the officer gaining on me.

I was done playing cat and mouse so I made a sharp cut into an alleyway and the cop fell right for my trap. As he put all his momentum into turning the corner, he slammed his face right into my elbow that met him with the same force.

A huge crack sent the officer down to the ground hard.

"AHH, you broke my nose." he shouted as he held his face in agony.

I could see his face was flat as I had completely shattered the man's nose. I stood over him. My feet were level with his chest as I looked down at this inferior man. The power I felt at this moment was exhilarating. How could I be feeling this when my wife just died five minutes ago? 'What the heck's happening to me?' I finally snapped out of my trance and crouched down over the wounded officer. "Sorry officer. No hard feelings," I stated as I ran as fast as I could out of sight.

The officer clearly didn't try anything as his focus was on holding his nose, though he no longer had much of one.

I didn't slow down my escape as I ran through the alley and cut right across the main road, straight into the adjacent one. I ran and ran, never looking back to see if anyone else was chasing me.

I found a little bridge that stood over a small stream and I hid under it, keeping myself hidden in the darkness. I panted and tried to catch my breath, as I slowed down my breathing until it finally was under control again. I sat on the cold snow and laid my back against the wall of the underpass. The exhaustion I was feeling was overpowering and everything that was happening around me was not enough to keep me awake. I tried to fight it but soon I was at the mercy of sleep and my eyes shut, still burning until I dozed off.

I slept for possibly a few hours as the sun was now creeping through the cloudy sky. I didn't want to stay in one spot too long to avoid being seen by any officers. I had to make my way as close to the main streets to assess the officers' methods of capturing me. I came from under the overpass, as I hugged my short jacket tightly against my chest. I made my way up a nearby alley and climbed a wooden stairwell to the roof of the building. I could hear the gathering of cops on the intersections as I watched from the edge of the roof overlooking the city street.

Jesus, I wonder if Joseph had heard the news yet? Or even poor Susan and John. If Joseph actually believed the cops I was a dead man. Knowing my luck, I would have all of the Irish searching for me by the afternoon.

What could I do to kill Vlad? Suddenly the light bulb lit up again. I swear I had no idea this bulb even worked anymore since I couldn't even get a job. But since the nightmare that had just happened it was like my animal instincts were taking over me. What if Vlad was the one that set me up all along? This would be just another reason to kill him. Putting me in prison for murder meant I would be hung and he would kill Evelyn clearing all trace of me from existence, a good way of paying the debt I owed him.

I was feeling drowsy again. I sat against the edge of the roof inside the stairwell that led into the building. I felt my eyes shutting once more.

As I woke up drooling down my cheek, I looked up to the smog filled sky of New York City. The coal used in refineries and trains made dark clouds over the city. People from other states would always talk about how disgusting our sky looked, but it wasn't bad. One would get used to it after living here for a few weeks.

Thankfully, the stairwell gave me protection from the wind chill that was rolling through, but hell was I frozen. I actually looked down at my feet and hands just to make sure they were still there and hadn't broken off in my sleep. I got on my feet slowly and made my way to the roof's edge once more to look down at the city street some twenty feet below me. There they were more organized then ever — officers stationed all around the streets in pairs. Luckily for me it was a regular day in New York and there were thousands of people buying food and doing their business. It would be my perfect opportunity to blend in with the crowd for my escape.

As I contemplated my next move, I continued to watch the officers stroll along the street, and notice there patterns. From the thousands of faces out there, I don't know how I was able to spot him but I did. There he was; Detective Owen Murphy leading the charge against me. I almost envied the guy at how sure he was of his talent. You could see it in the way he walked.

I needed a newspaper badly to figure out what their plan was.

I made my way downstairs, which took me a while since the hallways were crowded with the hundreds of immigrant inhabitants that lived there. It's actually really disgusting to think that forty-five people could live in one room with a capacity for six. Three floors with six rooms on each floor meant a lot of people under one roof. This was the only way immigrants could come to our land and survive here. To them it was still an amazing new life. You could see it in their faces, a beautiful opportunity which in truth was not.

I would rather pay the higher rent and live alone with Evel.. my beloved.. I could no longer hold it anymore as everything that happened hit me over the head like a ton of bricks. I began sobbing. The pain was too much to bear at the thought of her never coming back into my arms. I stopped a few steps from the front door and leaned against the wall, crouching down and holding my head with my hands as I cried, feeling deep pain.

Evelyn being really ill lately and me losing my job at the councilor's office made our lives spiral out of control, which put us in desperate need of money. That's where Vlad came in. Too bad the money he gave me went all for us to eat and pay for medical expenses. When it was time to pay rent, there was none. Let's not even get into paying him back. That was definitely impossible.

I made my way out the front door and saw two officers coming towards me, so I hid back inside and waited for them to pass. I stuck my head out and saw that the coast was clear so I pushed my jacket half way up my face and quickly made my way down the street. I turned the corner and there it was— the newsstand. The person selling the newspapers was no more than eleven years of age. You could tell the kid had emigrated from another land, as his accent was obvious. It was a smart way of the newspaper companies selling the paper, while paying a child peanuts. This child was making no more than thirty cents a week, but to him it was plenty.

The boy noticed me and he shouted. "Hey there, Sir. I see you eyeballing the paper. Come get one here for five cents."

Dammit, this fool was putting too much attention on me. I really hoped the kid would look away because I was sure my face was on the paper. I needed to get out of here quick. I reached into my pocket and I could feel the brass touch my fingers. I grasped the coin, pulled it out and there it was— a nickel. I tossed it to the boy, with my head down to the ground, and he caught it.

"Hey there, fella. Thanks for the coin. Enjoy the paper," the boy shouted to me excitingly.

I never took my eyes off the ground. I grabbed the paper and pulled it over my face as I rushed into the nearest alleyway.

My heart raced as I looked through the pages and there it was. 'One hundred dollar reward for the alive capture of wanted fugitive Lawrence Talbot.' They even managed to put a picture of me with Evelyn at the celebration of the fourth of July two years ago.

"Alright focus, Lawrence. Come on," I told myself as I looked down at the details: 'Mr. Lawrence Talbot is extremely dangerous. We will have cops patrolling the streets in pairs set up around each of the intersections until we can apprehend the criminal.'

Joseph was definitely going to come looking for me now that I was in the paper. I didn't care about dying but not before Vlad got what was coming to him first. I dropped the newspaper where I was standing and quickly snuck my way through the alleyway. It would place me right across the street from my home. I had run a big circle and had ended where I started.

As I stepped out onto the street, I looked around for officers but the coast was clear. I quickly made my way to the front steps and noticed the door was open. I made myself welcome and walked inside. I was hoping to get the seven dollars I had in my cupboard to buy a weapon to rid myself of my problem. I also needed a new change of clothes since all this blood would definitely attract way too much attention to me.

As I walked into what was my home just hours before, something unexpected happened that I had not anticipated. Ben Johnson, the only African American landlord on this street, was on his knees washing the blood from where Evelyn had died just a few short hours ago.

Ben looked over his shoulder thinking it was probably his wife or one of his kids but his facial reaction clearly showed me that he was not impressed at all to see me.

Ben grabbed the mop from his side and cracked it over his knee. His face was shocked and disgusted to see me. He dropped the fabric side of the mop to the ground and held the sharp wood towards me firmly with both hands.

"I'm going to kill you for Evelyn, you murderer! How could you? She was a sweet woman," Ben shouted angrily.

"Ben, I would never do this."

Ben didn't care to even hear anything I had to say. He just shot forward and tried to pierce my gut with the pointed edge. But I shot myself back away from the strike.

There it was again— the excitement I had when I stood over the defenseless officer. I had known Ben for a couple of years but that was all out the window now. I was a fugitive and if I let him go he would tell the officers that I had been here. At the same time if I killed him here than they were definitely going to know it was me since this was my apartment.

I quickly got out of deep thought as Ben came at me with his body weight screaming. He pressed me up against the wall. He was attempting to choke me with the stick as he pushed it to my throat, but a quick knee to the jewels solved that problem. Ben quickly retracted and curled up, revealing his face completely for my knee to make contact. I didn't hesitate. Ben was a good man but he was at the wrong place at the wrong time. I kneed the good man as hard as I could right in the face. Lucky for him, I grazed his nose and got more forehead then anything. It was still a hard blow as he stumbled to the ground flat on his back and the stick rolled off to the side of the room.

I stood there angrily watching him and the wooden stick. Ben and I both stared at each other and then the stick and we both went for it with all our might. Luckily for me, I was standing and it was much easier to get the weapon than Ben, who had to slither his way there. I stood over Ben now as he began to beg for his life.

"Please Lawrence— I'm sorry. I..I got kids. Please."

I was ready to kill Ben in a heartbeat but the mentioning of kids made me lose my rage. I hadn't even totally acknowledged that I had lost my child too. I think it must have had to do with the fact that it was still news to me recently and I was still shocked.

I was on a dark path with nowhere to escape. I could feel the darkness swallowing me whole but I wasn't ready to kill an innocent man just to get away. I dropped the stick and made my way to the door.

As I reached the door, I looked back over my shoulder, saying softly, "I'm sorry, Ben. I didn't mean to hurt you."

"I know, Lawrence" Ben said as he got up to his feet.

I completely turned around to see him holding the damn stick again.

"I can't let a killer walk these streets. You killed your wife. Just imagine who else you will kill," Ben said surely like he knew I was already a dead man. I was sorry for him but there was no way I was dying today.

He charged towards me, Even though I had shown him mercy, there was no way in hell I was going to do it again. I hated having to do this but the fool left me no choice.

As Ben tried to pierce me with the stick, I shifted over to the side letting his momentum trip him up. He stumbled over his own feet and crashed towards the wall. I quickly got behind him before he could maneuver himself, while yanking the stick out of his hand. Just as he was turning to gain back his footing, I drove the stick deep into his gut. Ben jerked and shuffled but the stick had done its job. I kept pressing the stick deeper and deeper with all my might until he sat flat on his ass. When his left leg stopped twitching, I knew he was dead.

As Ben lay dead by the front door, I stood over him feeling a great rush over me. It wasn't a good feeling; it was panic. I could feel myself starting to breathe rapidly as I stuck my head out into the hallway to see if anyone had heard the commotion. The coast was clear so I went back in and kicked Ben off to the side. He stumbled over and it gave me enough space to close the door.

I needed to change my clothes as I looked in the washroom mirror. I was covered in blood practically from head to toe now. I quickly tossed my clothes off and washed my hands and face with the bucket of water we had near the tub. I needed to change my appearance. Even though I loved my beard with all my heart, I went into the kitchen, grabbed a knife and took it all off. My hair sat comfortably on my shoulders but I also needed to take a few inches off. When I was done, I went over to my dresser and pulled out my newest clothes, which was a black long leather trench coat with a diamond design of stitching all along the back, a white shirt with a burgundy colored vest that had a floral design to it and a pair of black pants. I also grabbed my black top hat, which had a thin piece of the same material as the vest to match. I reached inside of it and pulled out the seven dollars I had collected in it. I put the money in my pocket, grabbed my finest knee high boots and put them on. There was no way the cops would be looking for me in nice clothing. It wouldn't make me invisible but my different appearance would help.

I made my way out the door and back out into the street. There were even more people out now, which made it easier to blend in as I made my way through the middle of the crowds. Every time cops were nearby, I would hunch myself over by a nearby vendor and act as if I was looking to purchase something. It was very easy to blend in now as I wasn't covered in all that blood. The top hat was also a great addition in hiding my face when I looked down at the ground.

I knew from this moment on I would never be able to go back to the way things were. I had killed a man. I was a fugitive on the run, and now I realized I had to get my hands on a gun.

CHAPTER 6: MURPHY'S GUN SHOP

I made my way down the street towards Murphy's Gun Shop, which were just a few blocks from my house. I could feel something pressing into my chest from the inside of my vest so I reached inside with my fingers to see what was it. It was a silver locket with a picture of Evelyn in it. My eyes began to tear and my heart pained for her. What I would do to hold her one last time in my arms. I wiped my eyes to better see her picture. I kissed the photo and placed it back in my vest.

As I smiled looking at the ground, I heard a commotion up ahead and saw two groups fighting with each other. The Five Point war was over more than two decades ago but the city still had many smaller gangs fighting for control of the underground activity. I didn't want to get in the mix of things, which would definitely draw too much attention to me, I cut my way through the next street and took the long way to the gun shop.

Just outside the gun shop, I looked around to see if I was being followed and again the coast was clear. I took a deep breath and opened the door as I made my way inside. There she was, a simple and pretty woman standing behind the counter. She was definitely the total opposite of what I thought I would encounter in here. I expected possibly a ruffian of a man with a navy grade rifle sitting at his side.

"Hey there, stranger," the gun owner said to me as we met eyes.

"Hey, yourself," I responded as I avoided eye contact and just shopped with my eyes at all the pistols. "I got seven bucks. What can I get with that?" I inquired firmly, but keeping my voice civil. I honestly wasn't in the mood for much talking.

The owner smiled and reached under the counter pulling out a beautifully crafted pistol. The long silver barrel showed much class with its engraved rose petal designs. The wooden handle made a nice touch to it and would help with the grip.

"This beautiful pistol is the Colt Model 1851 Navy. It's what you can get with your money. I can clearly tell you're not here to play games so that's why I pulled this baby out. Any fool that wants to stand in your way won't be standing there much longer when you pull this baby out," the owner explained confidently.

I could instantly tell this woman knew so much about weapons but I guess she had to since she owned a store full of them. It wasn't something you saw regularly since most women stayed at home with their children. It was actually nice to see a woman working a regular job.

"What about bullets?" I asked as I didn't see her pull any out.

"I'm just messing with you. Clearly you're a first timer," the owner said as she laughed aloud.

"What do you mean?" I quickly asked

"Guns aren't cheap. Seven bucks will buy you this," she said as she reached in her pocket and pulled out a silver switch blade, tossing it dangerously close to my hand that was rested on the countertop.

The blade stuck directly into the counter just an inch from my hand as I pulled myself back a foot.

"You come in here mocking me, thinking I'm a fool because I'm a woman," she said as she pulled out her Remington at her side and pointed it towards me. "I know who you are, Lawrence. Jeez, everyone knows who you are now," the gun owner said as she kept the pistol dead locked on my face. "Pull out the seven bucks you got, and toss em' on the counter. Then grab your blade and get out," she ordered.

I wanted to kill her where she stood but I was in no position to do anything except what she wanted. I reached into my pocket slowly and pulled out the money, dropping it on the counter slowly.

"I'm going to grab the blade," I said as I reached for it and put it in my jacket.

"I see you got a silver locket. Give it here," she ordered, waving her gun at me.

"Not a chance lady," I answered back abruptly without thought. My heart was pounding even harder and I knew this wasn't going to end well.

"Give it here or I'll blow you away. See it as payment for wasting my time," she insisted angrily.

I couldn't believe I had to give this bitch my locket of Evelyn just so I would survive another day. But this was New York and the strong preyed on the weak.

I reached for the locket with one hand while my other hand stayed up in the air. "At least tell me your name?" I asked trying to get her attention off my hands.

"Don't know why you would care but the name's Grace, Grace Murphy," she answered as she didn't even flinch.

Damn she was good. I had to find a way to distract her but then it hit me. I hoped to God I was wrong but her and the detective had the same last name. I then asked, "You're not related to Detective Murphy, are you?"

Grace cracked a sarcastic smile, "Oh but I am. He's my father."

How could this be happening to me? Of all the people that would own a gun shop, it had to be the detective's daughter. I had to make sure I got out of here alive but I couldn't kill her. I threw the locket hard at the owner and she flinched, giving me a chance to jump over the counter top and push her to the wall as hard as I could.

She was unarmed as she dropped her gun. I grabbed her as she tried to reach for her pistol and tossed her to my other side, distancing her from her weapon. I used my strength against her and tripped her to the ground as I got on top of her.

"Why didn't you just kill me if you knew it was me?" I asked.

Grace didn't fight back. She just answered, "I believe you're innocent."

We locked eyes and didn't move for a brief moment. I could see her looking at me oddly and then it happened; she kissed me.

I couldn't believe that one moment ago she was ready to take my head off and the next she was kissing me. I used this to my advantage. I went with it longer so she would put her guard down. I loved one woman and had no room in my heart for anyone else. I pulled the knife out of my pocket and pressed it against her throat.

Her eyes widened and she lay there still as I got up with my knife pointed towards her. I took her holster and pistol. "I need bullets. Where can I find them?" I asked her, but it was more of an order.

"It's there, the drawer by your left side," she said as she pointed to it still laid out on the ground.

I opened the drawer and pulled out a blue box showing it to her. "Is it these?" I asked.

She nodded at me.

I went over to the counter and dropped my blade, knowing she wasn't stupid enough to try something again. If she wanted me dead, I would have been already.

"Get up," I ordered and she did just that as she stood next to me.

I handed her gun back and grabbed the navy pistol. I pressed against the router and opened up the gun inserting bullets into it until it was fully loaded. I spun the router and closed the gun . I then tied the holster to my waist and put the gun at my side. I took the silver blade and put it back in my pocket. I grabbed another handful of bullets and also put them in my pocket.

"Listen, I appreciate you believing me. For what it's worth, I didn't do it," I explained

"So what happened then? I can help you," Grace insisted as she came closer to me.

"I don't need help now. I just need to avenge my wife," I said as boldly as I could. I tried to hold it but I felt my lower lip quiver.

"What happened? Who did this to your wife and child?"

"I made mistakes to people that don't tolerate error and instead of me paying for it, they hurt me the best way they could," I said as I crouched down and picked up the silver locket, placing it back in my vest.

"I can talk to my father. He's a good man. Believe me, he can help you."

"I believe your father is a good man," I said as I looked her in the eyes. "But your father has devoted his life to the law, and he will never believe my innocence."

"You don't know that."

"I DO." I shouted back in response. "I'm sorry I didn't mean to raise my voice. You have been kinder than most to me. You didn't deserve that."

"It's alright. You're under a lot of pressure," Grace responded calmly as she placed her hand on mine.

I looked down at her hand and could see my wedding ring's reflection through her index and middle finger. I felt calm at this moment, almost even safe. This Grace woman was treating me like a human being and it felt good.

The front door of the gun shop opened and Grace and I both looked to see who was entering. To my utter shock, Detective Owen Murphy walked in with his pistol pointed right at me. I quickly drew my pistol and we both were ready to kill the other.

CHAPTER 7: MR. VLAD REZNIK

"I told you we would keep in touch," the detective said aggressively. "Drop your weapon right now and get away from the woman."

"Oh you mean your daughter?" I asked sarcastically as I grinned.

I could see the detective tense up and quickly look at Grace then back at me.

"Dad, I told him who I am. Can we please put down the guns and talk this through in the back room?"

"Only if Papa here puts his down first," I said as I kept my gun ever focused on the detective's face.

"I would never lower my weapon to a killer."

"He's innocent dad, I'm telling you."

"Oh is he now? Well maybe there's a slight chance he is for his wife but he definitely murdered his landlord, or did he forget to mention that one?" the detective asked.

I glanced over my shoulder to see Grace's terrified face. I decided to lower my weapon and see where this conversation would lead me. I lowered my gun hoping that the detective would too but he kept his gun right on me.

"I'll confess in the back room, but no cops," I instructed as I holstered my gun, turned my back to both of them and walked into the little room. I could hear the two of them mumbling to each other and then Grace and her father walked in. I noticed Detective Murphy had his gun holstered, which released some of the tension.

"You're one hell of a man. Two interviews in eight hours," Detective Murphy said as he grabbed a chair for him and Grace.

I liked the idea so I also got one and planted myself hard on it. I was so exhausted and frozen that the warmth of the little room made me almost want to doze off.

"This is not an interview. This is a confession" I stated.

"That's even better for me."

"A confession.. Of who killed my wife" I cut in.

"Did you kill Mr. Ben Johnson?" Detective Murphy asked.

"I did, in self-defense."

"Is that so?" he asked again.

"I went back to my apartment to get fresh clothes. When I walked in, Ben my landlord was mopping up my wife's blood." I could feel my damn lip quivering again. I didn't want to show weakness.

"So he was cleaning Mrs. Talbot's blood and then what, he saw you and attacked?"

"That's exactly what happened. I even knocked him down and tried leaving but he came back again and left me no choice."

"Mr. Talbot, there's always a choice, like turning yourself in."

I looked over at Grace. "I told you he would not listen to my statement."

Grace whispered in her father's ear.

"Alright, my apologies. So you killed him in self-defense, which I will personally go to the apartment and see if your story adds up." The detective was getting upset as he rose from his chair and approached me. "What I don't understand is how you could be falsely accused of three murders. Don't forget Tom Finagin. People must really want you out of the picture."

"I was set up for Tom's death, which was a distraction for my loan shark to get my wife."

"Loan shark?" I could see Detective Murphy's eyes widen.

"You borrowed money?"

"Have you seen today's society? Everything is expensive and at the time I didn't imagine getting money to keep my family alive would end up biting me in the ass and getting them killed instead."

The detective just stood there thinking about something.

"Dad, did you hear him?" Grace asked. I had forgotten she was even in the room since she had been silent for quite some time.

"Uhh.. yeah.. the shark, he wouldn't by any chance go by the name of Vlad Reznik?"

"Yes, that's the son of a bitch!" I shouted even louder than I had anticipated.

"I have been looking for that man for a long time. Well your story checks out. Vlad is not a person many people even know so I'm now sure you're telling the truth."

Grace smiled from ear to ear.

I didn't feel content. Just because I was free didn't mean I wanted to leave Vlad and his goons to the law. They would be dealt justice by me.

"Unfortunately for you, the Johnson family needs closure, and that means I'm going to have to arrest you for Ben Johnson's murder," the detective said as he took the cuffs from his pocket.

"Dad but you heard him" Grace said trying to change her father's mind.

"Silence," the detective ordered as he looked back at his daughter.

I realized I was in the same boat I was in just a few minutes ago, and so I took the opportunity of his distraction to tackle the detective to the ground. We stumbled into a table and crashed hard against the back wall. I quickly got back to my feet and unholstered my gun, pointing it at him.

"Don't you move. I swear I'll blow your knee clean off," I said. I wasn't kidding. I was back into survival mode. "Get up and sit on that chair. Grace I need you to get me some rope," I ordered.

Grace hesitated so I made sure she focused. "Grace, rope, now."

Grace ran into the other room.

"You're never going to get away from me, this is my city and I will catch you. I just hope you don't bury yourself in a deeper hole. Leave the justice to the cops, Mr. Talbot," the detective said as he propped the chair back and sat on it.

Grace entered the room with some rope.

"Tie your father," I ordered again.

She tied her father tightly to the chair and then waited to know what of her.

"Take the other chair and sit back to back with him," I ordered.

Grace did just as I told her. I grabbed the rest of the rope and tied her arms behind the chair. I spun the rope around them both, making sure they were both going to be occupied for some time.

I don't know why I was feeling what I was feeling but I reached in and kissed Grace on the cheek and then whispered to her, "I'm sorry."

I walked out of the room and could instantly hear them fidgeting their way loose, so I sprinted out the door and down the street.

I was never very religious but I felt as though I needed to go see my old friend and confess what I was going to do. I headed towards the church. It had been a long time.

CHAPTER 8: AN OLD FRIEND

After an hour of walking I made it to the church. I walked through the side door on the east end of the building and waited to literally erupt in a ball of flames for killing Ben. Obviously nothing happened as that would clearly be ridiculous, but I had my superstitious moments. I wanted to confess what I had done to Ben. I didn't want to kill him but he left me no choice. That little bit of my religious self, yearned for Father Edwards and I was willing to see him.

Father Edwards was having his early evening mass so I crept my way to the back of the church, and waited for him to finish. I had known Father Edwards since I was a young boy. My parents were very religious and used to come to church every Sunday to hear the mass and practice their religion. Me, I was never very religious. Sure I do believe there's something more out there but I don't like getting into the whole practice and strong belief. My belief was that what comes around goes around. Me killing Ben would definitely come to bite me in the ass someday and I would accept it, just not until my vengeance was at an end— if there ever was one.

As the mass finished, I made my way slowly to the front of the church near the altar. I could see Father Edwards saying his goodbyes to the folks as they went up to him one by one. I noticed him look down at me with widened eyes and then look around to see if anyone else had noticed me. Each time someone came to bid the good father farewell, he would say to them 'Go with god' and then throw me a quick glance to see if I was still there.

After a good five minutes, the father had said goodbye to everyone, as most people had left the church. There were a couple of stragglers, mostly old folks that liked to hang around for a while after the mass was over to do their extra prayers.

Father Edwards made his way down the altar, bee lining it towards me but also keeping his cool to not attract attention and grabbed me by the arm.

"Hello there, son of God. Let us go to confession," Father addressed me, but it was more like an order. Father brought me to the confessional booth and guided me in— more like tossed me inside.

Father sat at his booth and pulled his face close to the fencing that divided the priest and the person confessing their sins.

"Lawrence, I need you to tell me what happened? Tell me this is all a misunderstanding."

"I have been framed, Father."

"I knew it. I couldn't believe you had done something so awful as to kill a person."

I cleared my throat as I thought of Ben. What was the easiest way of confessing what I had done. Hell, there was no easy way so I just let it out softly. Well.. I did kill someone, just not my beloved, Evelyn."

I could feel the tension coming from Father Edwards. "Why would you kill a man? There is no space in Heaven for killers, Lawrence."

"I understand that, but I don't need God right now. I need you, my friend."

"Without God, my son, you cannot expect to live a peaceful life. I know you're angry, and you have every right to be, but murder is not going to bring Evelyn back to you," Father Edwards said wholeheartedly.

I was beginning to feel irritated. "Father, I will never have peace until the people who took my beloved are dealt with."

Father Edwards was silent for a moment and then spoke calmly," If you're not looking for God's help then why would you come to church?"

"I feel as if I am losing my reason. I feel as if I could kill anyone. I feel so lost," I said as I began to cry.

"Lawrence, God works in mysterious ways and though the death of Evelyn seems impossible to live with, in time you will. Just don't go doing things that you may someday regret. Let God punish the sinners. You stay focused on God and being his shepherd," Father Edwards said calmly.

"Father, do you believe that holy water could calm my soul, when it beckons for blood?" I can't believe I asked him that. If this was just twenty four hours before all this mess happened I would have thought I was going crazy— but I wasn't. I felt an evil inside lurking in my heart that had an unquenchable thirst for blood.

Father Edwards didn't answer. He just got out of the booth. I quickly got to my feet and walked out to meet him. He had his hands together in a form of prayer while his eyes met mine.

"If you feel like you need this water to help you, I will give it to you. But know that the water cannot wash away your guilt. Your brain is just playing tricks on you and its finding a way to protect itself from the tragedy you experienced. By you going out there and murdering other people it will only make your pain increase tenfold when you realize what you're doing. Your soul mourns, and you want answers, and I'm telling you son, not as a priest but as your friend, stay here with me and I will help you through this."

Father Edwards then turned around and made his way to the altar.

Could I really be making up stories in my mind? There was no way in hell I was going to believe that. I would kill everyone who got in my way.

Father Edwards then came to me with a small glass bottle of holy water.

"Here's the holy water. Now would you like to come get some food in your system, and maybe a shower?" Father asked me as he gave me a look as if I stunk.

"Alright," I said as I followed him to the back behind the altar. The father's chamber was nice; it had elegant decor to decorate the place, It was small but felt cozy, a place that could definitely feel like home.

Father reached into a cupboard and pulled out a cloth, "The bathroom is there. Clean yourself up and I'll prepare supper for you."

I reached in and grabbed the cloth from Father's hand. "Thanks Father," I said with a low grin.

"You don't need to thank me. You're always welcome here," he responded as he walked over to the kitchen four feet away.

I stepped into the washroom and began to undress. I then washed the horrible day off me. I felt refreshed as I came out with the cloth practically wrapped around my face as I finished drying my hair.

The first thing I noticed when I stepped out was the smell of stew. I looked down at the table ahead of me and there was a bowl of bean stew still steaming, just made. "Where was the priest?" I pondered to myself. I walked around the bend of his home and creeped my head out over the altar to see Father Edwards speaking to the woman I met back at the station. It was Detective Murphy's partner, Annie.

Damn, did Father actually call the police?' That had to be impossible. I was certain he would never backstab me. But I continued to peek anyway.

I waited as I noticed Annie thanking the father. She bowed her head to him as she made her way out of the church. At that moment I knew Father Edwards was the only person I could trust. He didn't sell me out. He actually protected me knowing I had killed a man. I met the priest half way through the entrance and he nearly jumped out of his skin in fear.

"Sorry for alarming you," I said as I chuckled

"My Lord, son, don't ever do that again. You trying to kill me?" the good father asked as he returned a chuckle and we walked back into his room.

I sat at the table and began to literally inhale the stew.

"Careful, Lawrence, it's hot," Father Edwards said to me as he sat across from me at the table.

My mouth was full but I didn't care as I responded to his advice. "Thanks, but it's just fine," I quickly said as I finished the stew.

"I gotta ask you kid, who did this to Evelyn?"

"I owed money to the wrong people, Father. She...she was pregnant."

Father's jaw dropped as he quickly got back to his feet and came around the table, placing his hand on my shoulder. "I'm so sorry, Lawrence," Father said as he grabbed the back of my neck and reached in for a kiss on my forehead.

I accepted the kiss and then looked up at him. "I owed money and to make me suffer they killed her and our child in front of me. They made me watch as they gut her like a pig." I grinded my teeth in anger, my nostrils flared and I took huge breathes of air.

"I hope you can find it in your heart to turn yourself in so God can forgive you for your sins. Please don't run around searching for these dangerous killers. You're only going to get yourself killed." I know that Father cared for me but I didn't have time to chat, or sleep —I had to leave. I got up on my feet and put my top hat on. I reached in close and hugged Father as hard as I could. "I'm not crazy and I know what I'm doing, but you're mistaken with something."

Father looked at me in the eyes waiting to hear what I had to say.

"People will die, but I will not be on that list. Good day Father," I said as I made my exit out of the church.

I quickly made my way out to the street and waited nearby, behind a chariot. The chariot was on the side of the road with crates of lettuce stacked up to the top. It was good to know Father could be trusted when I needed somewhere to lay low if things got out of hand.

My entire evening consisted of stealing a few apples and hiding in the darkest corners until morning arrived. I wanted to know where Evelyn was going to be buried. Evelyn's funeral would come to pass today if everything went smoothly, so I went near the Bakers residence.

CHAPTER 9: FUNERAL

As I watched the Bakers residence from a nearby shop window, I could see Conor and some of Joseph's goons outside the home waiting for him while he was inside with his parents. Evelyn's parents were good people. I felt dearly for their loss. I wish I could speak with them and give them the closure they needed. I knew Evelyn's death would destroy them since she was practically all they had. Joseph only came around in times of tragedy or once a year for supper like he did the night before.

Joseph lived for the Forty Thieves. Evelyn loved him but I really didn't like it when he was around because his goons would stare at her like she was a piece of meat, especially that bastard Conor.

I could see Detective Murphy making his way out the door of the Bakers residence with Annie to his left. They both hopped on the chariot and rode down the street. Murphy was probably paying his respects to the family, and hopefully filling them in on the events of Evelyn's murder. I would never let Vlad get caught by Murphy. I had to kill him myself. I would get my revenge for Evelyn and leave New York, never to return. There was honestly nothing left for me here.

I probably stood in the same damn spot for over an hour until finally I could see Joseph coming out with his parents. Joseph's bald head was easy to spot from a distance. He looked more Irish than American, the way he dressed and walked. His goons helped the parents down the steps while Joseph tried to compose himself. I could see the anger in his posture. He definitely wanted blood. I'm guessing detective Murphy hadn't filled the family in on his discovery during our conversation.

Joseph had a carriage waiting by the edge of the road. As soon as he gave the signal, a chariot charged from around the corner street and pulled up in front of the house. Conor opened the door so John, Susan, and Joseph could step inside. I quickly hurried up the outside steps to the nearest building's roof as I was going to follow on foot. Me living on the streets had made me exhausted but I would climb from building to building until I saw where my beloved would rest for eternity.

The chariot began to go down the street and I quickly made my way from building to building, jumping the roofs as quickly as I could. Deep down inside, I knew that Evelyn would be buried at the Trinity Church Cemetery. It was a fairly new cemetery and that's where the middle class were mostly laid to rest. I could not make assumptions, I needed to be certain and that's why I pursued steadily.

I jumped from building to building, almost stumbling to my death a few times. I didn't contemplate the risks I was in as I was no more than an animal on a dark path of revenge. When animals are fixated on something, they don't think of anything else except their goals and I definitely felt that rush.

The chariot turned north on Riverside and I was forced to jump from the roof into one of the lower apartment windows. As I smashed through the glass, I came to a sudden halt when I cracked through someone's dining room table. A woman and her children screamed in horror.

"Get out!" shouted the woman frantically as she grabbed a pot and tossed it at me.

"Sorry," I shouted back as I opened the door to the outside and avoided catching the pot to the face.

I ran on foot down the street while panting in deep exhaustion now. My entire left side throbbed from the fall but I continued to push on thinking of nothing but keeping up with the chariot. Every step that hit the ground felt like a thousand knives at my side.

A chariot delivering bread made a sudden turn my way and I leaped onto it's back as stealthily as I could. I hung on tightly as I rose up and squinted to see if the rider had noticed me. The rider was focused on his business and didn't notice the extra weight on his ride. I looked out past him to see the Bakers still going up Riverside Street.

After a few blocks, the bread chariot made a right turn and I leaped off, rolling onto the dirt road. As I wiped the dirt off my jacket, I continued to run. I could see the cemetery and the Bakers pulling up behind the chariot that carried my beloved Evelyn. I snuck behind a building's side wall and kept my eye on the family. From down Riverside, a dozen chariots came charging together with officers on each. I rushed back, blending myself in with some folk that were hanging out on the street.

All the chariots pulled up behind the Bakers in one line. Detective Murphy and Annie his assistant, approached the family and they all went in together. Detective Murphy was too brilliant and I didn't like it, the bastard knew I would be here.

I made my way slowly down the street. As two cops that were guarding the entrance looked at me, I nodded my head and turned on the street heading away from the site. As I looked back, I noticed the officers were no longer paying attention and so I quickly crossed the street and hopped the wall into the graveyard. I hid behind a tree as I watched everyone gather, and four men bring my beloved in her casket to the burial site. As the men set the casket down, everyone waited silently. No one spoke; just sobs could be heard from Evelyn's entire family. Then after a few moments Father Edwards, appeared as he came towards the site and began to say a prayer for the deceased.

Father Edwards was going to say the prayer for the funeral and he didn't even tell me? Unless, deep down he believed I didn't murder Evelyn and so he didn't want me coming here to get caught. He knew that if he told me where she was going to be, I wouldn't resist coming. I guess Father doesn't know me as well as he thinks he does because here I am.

After Father Edwards was done speaking, he called up Detective Owen Murphy. I got closer and hid behind some poor soul's tombstone to hear what the detective had to say. The detective stood beside Evelyn's casket while Annie stood by his side.

"Hello everyone. For whomever doesn't know me, I'm Detective Owen Murphy, and this is my assistant Annie Wilson from the New York Precinct. I'm going to keep this simple as I don't want to flood more things on top of you as grieving is very difficult. I thought I would take this time to inform you all that we now have the conclusive proof we needed to address that Evelyn's husband, Lawrence— is the killer. We have evidence that puts him at the crime scene of Evelyn Talbot, Tom Finagin, and Ben Johnson's murders. Lawrence went back the following morning, after killing his wife and Mr. Finagin, to get a fresh change of clothes and killed his landlord Mr. Johnson. Unfortunately, that is not all. He has struck a gun shop downtown. The owner, my daughter, says he is carrying an 1851 Colt navy pistol and is extremely armed and dangerous."

That two faced son of a gun. He didn't believe me, and to top it all off, he forgets to address the fact that he was at the shop.

I could see the disgust in everyone's faces.

"Please know we are doing everything in our power to find Lawrence and bring him to justice. Thank you and take care," Detective Murphy said as he made his way out of the cemetery with Annie and a group of officers.

I waited as everyone slowly made their way out of the cemetery.

When the coast was clear, I made my way over to Evelyn's tombstone. Which was elegantly crafted. The tombstone had a rose carved into it with a dove flying over.

I knelt beside the tombstone and felt the soft wet soil hug my knee.

"My Evelyn, I wanted to come and see you, to know where you would rest forever. I'm so sorry I couldn't protect you and I know you said for me not to blame myself, but I always will. Until I get revenge for your murder, I will kill all three of them."

I then reached in and kissed the tombstone as passionately as one can kiss cement. I could see the tears dripping from my face as they fell onto the wet soil and tombstone. I got back up and slowly turned around as I could see three cops running towards me.

They blew their whistles to alert nearby officers as they ran through the cemetery to catch me. There wasn't much I could do, except kill them all. I ran into a catacomb entrance without a second thought. It was dark and had many corridors I could hide in. The only way I was going to make it out of this alive was for me to separate the cops and then kill them one by one. I was done wasting time and anyone that came in my way would die. There was no time for remorse or pity. I had to keep moving forward, which meant keep killing.

I turned into multiple corridors, switching from right to left and left to right. Surely the cops were as lost as I was.

I could hear their footsteps through the echo of the corridor. I peeked around the corners before moving around. As I stuck my head out, I saw Annie Wilson. I knew cops were chasing me but I didn't take the time to see who they were exactly. That gave me a pretty good shot that Detective Murphy was down here also. I had to be extra cautious. I pulled out my knife and held it firmly as I saw Annie coming towards me.

She walked right by me but didn't notice me as I let her slip through the corridor unharmed. I controlled my breathing calmly, not making noise as I waited in the shadows for my victim. The two cops came out side by side looking through each corridor as they walked by searching for me. This was good. Annie was leading the charge, which meant without Detective Murphy here I could escape. A part of me wanted to kill Annie but I felt I owed her for saving me during the interrogation the first time I met Detective Murphy. Then again it had nothing to do with her freeing me with the goodness of her heart.

I let the cops slip by and I came out from the shadows. The cops heard me and both turned around with their pistols ahead of them. I slashed my knife across one of the cop's throats. He dropped his gun and grabbed his throat with all his life, collapsing to the ground. The other cop shot his pistol towards me but missed as I dove at him and stabbed him in the chest. The officer tried to fight me off but I turned the blade and he gasped for air. The blood splashed out of his mouth with every breath as I could feel his power slipping away. The officer's knees buckled and we dropped to the ground. He looked at me with emptiness in his eyes, and I returned the gaze with a straight face.

I looked at the other officer and he had died already, still with his hands near his throat. This time there was no excitement. There was no nausea, or shaking, or feeling sick. There was nothing. Killing was easy now, and it was just for survival. I could hear Annie's footsteps charging towards my direction and instead of hiding and letting her escape, I wanted her to find me. I stood up in the open corridor still with the bloody knife in my hand. My pistol was holstered. Annie turned the corner and looked down in horror as her fellow officers were slain at my feet.

"You monster," she bickered at me in disgust.

For some odd reason I smiled. It was amusing looking at this woman in fear. Annie raised her gun and without a second thought, I threw the blade in her direction and pierced her stomach. I took a chance with that throw but luckily for me I got her. Annie turned around slowly as she looked at the knife that had punctured her stomach and began to walk over to the wall as she pulled the knife out and collapsed to one knee.

I walked over to her and stood above her. She had no more fight in her as she didn't even look at me. She just kept facing the ground as she tried holding me back with her hand raised in my direction. I unholstered my pistol and looked at it. A great joy came over me as I was excited to have my first kill with my pistol. I pointed the gun right to Annie's head and then I heard her faint whisper, "Please don't kill me."

I cocked the gun back and blew her brains all over the wall at point blank distance. The blood splat all over my jacket, boots, and face, as her body hunched over violently. I was done feeling anything for anyone. I was dead inside my heart, and now I was dead inside my soul, the perfect combo for retribution. I knew it was time to make my way over to the lion's den, the Five Points where I could find Vlad, and show him who the true monster was.

CHAPTER 10: ALIVE AGAIN

The last time I was in the Five Points, I had to meet Joseph when I was in need of money a few months ago. Joseph had told me he heard of a loan shark named Vlad and that's when I met the fool.

I wanted to keep the element of surprise on my side so that I could assure everything worked out. I hung out in the Five Points waiting to see if I could spot him or his guards, but they were nowhere to be seen. The evening was starting to bring more cold air and that meant that the streets were going to empty out. My element of surprise was no longer going to happen. I needed to act quickly and find him before then. I noticed a man robbing an elderly woman and then running for the alley. When he turned the corner, he stopped adjacent to me just across the street as he grinned and looked into her bag. The lady wept but couldn't chase the culprit. At this point, there was barely anyone on the street, and most folks just wanted to stay out of trouble. Lucky for her, I was feeling generous.

I approached the thug now leaning on a wall. "You know where I can find a Vlad?" I asked as I got uncomfortably close, making him nervous.

"Why don't you piss off. I never heard of no Vlad," the thug said angrily as he spat at my feet.

I didn't say a word but hell did I want to stab him in the neck. I just gave him a serious look. I wanted to provoke him. I wanted to kill someone again. I wanted to kill everyone that was garbage for the city; and this thug was garbage.

The thug edged up off the wall and got in my face. I could tell he had more rotting teeth than good ones as his breath was the same as the horse crap that was on the floor just two feet away.

"Listen here man, you turn around and walk or I'll shiv you," the thug said, trying to put fear in me." The problem was I was fresh out of fear for anything.

"No, you listen here," I said as I edged up closer to his face. "Take a walk with me and just try to SHIV me" I instigated and the thug fell right for it.

"Lead the way," the thug said with a smile on his face.

We made our way deeper into the alley way and he instantly pulled out his little switch blade. I, on the other hand, took no weapon out. I wanted the thrill of this moment. Killing Annie with the pistol was too simple. I needed a challenge this time around. My heart began to pound frantically in my chest and I just grinned towards the thug.

"You won't be laughing soon," the thug said as he began swaying his blade crazily at me. I reached in when he pulled back from a swing and grabbed his wrist. As he tried to pull himself off me, I used the momentum to pull him in and head butt him right in the face. He clearly didn't expect that and in one hit he was mine. He dropped the blade and I pulled him with my forearm against his throat to the wall. I reached in and bit his ear with all my strength. He screamed and roared in agonizing pain but I didn't submit. I could feel his warm blood filling my mouth almost to the point of gagging. To avoid choking, I yanked on his ear still with a clenched jaw and tore it clean off.

"Don't make me ask you again where that shit Vlad is," I demanded.

"Alright, alright," the thug quivered in fear and pain. He held the hole in the side of his head where his ear had been, trying to apply pressure to the wound. The thug attempted to speak through his quivering lips. "You can find him across the street at the Miller's Refinery. You probably won't be able to get near him as he has his two guards with him at all times." I could tell the man was about to pass out as his face was white as the snow on the ground.

"Thanks for the info, but leave how I get Vlad to me," I said as I pulled out my knife and stabbed the thug in the leg.

"Ah hell, let me go Mister, please!" he shouted as he grabbed his leg.

I left the bloody mess of a thug instantly and walked over to the edge of the alley towards the street now holding the purse. I handed the purse to the old woman. As she thanked me, I just walked away. I could see the Miller's Refinery sitting no more then thirty steps ahead of me.

I could see Evelyn being murdered in front of me over and over again in my head, and Vlad standing above her as she bled out.

I couldn't wait to get my vengeance but I would put it on hold for a moment. I approached the alley again and looked at the thug who was limping his way down towards the other end. He was mine, but it would have to be silent. If I shot this man, the echo would surely give me away. I pulled my knife out and ran towards the fleeing thug.

The thug turned around and watched me in terror as I ran at him with a cold stare. He froze in fear and then tried to break for it, but thankfully I had stabbed him in the leg and there was no way he would get away from me. The ravine just ahead had a narrow but long staircase to the bottom and he began going down the steps as I approached him. I easily caught up and kicked him down the steps with all my might. He cried and yelled as his body made hard contact with each and every step until the ground stopped his body.

I walked down the steps slowly enjoying the hunt. Evelyn dying had awoken something dormant inside of me that I would have never thought possible existed. I liked killing people. I liked the power and rush it gave me. I approached the man as he was dragging his body across the dirt.

"Please, I told you what you wanted to know. Spare me, man. I beg you. I got a kid," he said as he laid on his back and begged with his arms extended fully.

Children were no longer an excuse not to kill someone. I had knife kills, I had a pistol kill, now I wanted something different. I looked around but didn't find anything useful, just a rock which was boring, and the ravine. The latter seemed more enjoyable. I grabbed the man by the collar and dragged him to the water.

"Please don't!" the desperate man begged but I didn't give a fuck.

I grabbed him by the neck and dunked his head under. He flailed and danced around but he could not find the energy to get up. I had my knee sitting all my weight right on his spine. Even an ox of a man would have a hard time getting up. The flailing slowed, the fighting stopped and soon there was only the sound of the ravine. I closed my eyes, still holding the man submerged, and took a big breathe of air into my lungs. I then let him go and made my way back up the steps.

I made my way back onto the street. "Finally sweetheart" I said out loud as I began walking at a quick pace towards the entrance of the Refinery. This time anything went— rocks, water, pistol, knife. I didn't care as long as they died.

As I was going to step in, I veered my sight just to the left of the building and I could see the bastard that tried to smother my breathing when his partner tackled me down. My first target was in sight and I was ready to kill again. This time my heart pounded. Evelyn would be avenged.

My whole life had changed as I went from being a madly in love married man to a revenge seeking killer. I was going to kill this man and I wouldn't lose sleep at night.

I waited for Vlad's guard to finish talking to the lady he was conversing with, and then I saw him slip money towards her. Nice, buying a prostitute right in the open, classy.

They both walked for a while and then went where I assumed was her place as she was the one to open the door. I waited for a moment and then made myself welcome as I could hear them giggling upstairs. I crept my way up and saw them kissing in the hallway. The pig had his hands far up into her dress and was kissing her neck. That made me remember the good times when I made love to my sweet Evelyn.

Could I really be such a monster if I still had good memories? I would like to think that I was good, just because I killed to make sure I saw my wife avenged didn't make me heartless. The killing would stop as soon as Vlad was dead. Then there was the thug just a moment ago. I couldn't think about that now— I had to focus.

Watching this man kissing the prostitute was aggravating me but I had to be patient. I couldn't lose my focus on what was more important; not getting myself killed.

After a couple of minutes of groping, they finally went inside the apartment. I gave them time to get comfortable. I made my way to the door and unholstered my pistol. I cocked the gun back and with all my might kicked the door in.

The two 'love birds' were startled as they were half naked and looked at the door where I was pointing the gun straight at them.

"What the hell?" the guard said as he recognized me. "Hold on, don't hurt me. I will take you to Vlad."

"Now that's a true friend. You gave up Vlad without me even saying a word. Pitiful. Honey get dressed, and get out before you get involved in this." I addressed the whore and she quickly grabbed her things and made her way to the door.

"Hey where are you going with my money?" the guard shouted.

The woman looked back at me waiting for my instruction.

I responded, "Keep it for the troubles. Believe me he won't need it."

She took a big gulp and made her quick exit out the door.

I made my way in slowly, never taking my eye off the beast of a man. Well on the outside he was more like a quivering dog. It was actually sad to see.

"Listen man w…" he tried to say something but I was having none of it.

"Silence!" I shouted to stop him from talking.

He just looked at me as I sat at the kitchen table with the gun pointed at him.

"Sit at the other side of this table," I ordered and he got up in his briefs and made his way to the chair. He hesitated to sit, with fear, but I pointed for him to sit with the long intimidating barrel of my Colt pistol. He finally took a seat and just looked at me.

I took the gun and still pointing it towards him, placed it on my lap.

"Vlad tells me what to do. It's nothing personal."

"Is that so?" I asked rhetorically. there was nothing this fool could say that would make me spare him.

I pulled out my knife and opened the blade. The man looked at me in confusion as I placed it in front of him on the table.

"Now I'm going to let you decide how this is plays out," I said as I got comfortable for the show, but still had my pistol aimed at his stomach under the table.

"Look you want money? I got money. What you say I give you five hundred and you let me go? This way you pay your debt to Vlad and move on with your life."

"My life stopped moving on when my wife was murdered. Now interrupt me again and I'll gut you like a pig."

The guard's eyes nearly bulged out of their sockets as I could see the cold sweat coming down his face.

"Like I was saying before, you're going to decide what happens here. You have to choose either I kill you, or you take that knife and cut your right hand off."

"What are you crazy? I can't."

"Oh but you can. You wanted to smother me with your right hand so now you trade it for your life. It's that simple." I could see him contemplating what to do next as the sweat trickled down his forehead and into his mouth. The foul taste of sweat reminded him of his anxiety as he blinked quickly and then spat the sweat out. His eyes were fixated on the knife.

"Jesus Christ," the guard said as he placed his hand out in front of him, his forearm pressed to the table. He stabbed the knife right into his wrist and screamed as he tried to contain himself. The blood instantly pooled on the table as he began very slowly to take the knife and saw his wrist. After a minute his hand detached from the wrist and he let go of the knife and sobbed.

BAM! I shot him right in the stomach.

He gasped for air but clearly couldn't find it.

What, did he expect me to spare him? I was done wasting time.

I quickly rose up and made my way around the table as I could see he had pissed himself, probably from the hand being decapitated and not the gunshot. I grabbed the man by the hair and reached in close. "You thought you would get away with holding me, while Vlad killed my wife?" I shouted in his face as he tensed up from me tugging on his hair.

"I'm sorry, I swear," the man was sobbing more then a child that really wanted that special toy but couldn't have it.

"I'm not sorry," I responded quickly as I slammed his face into the table. The blood came like a river out of his mouth. The second slam against the table revealed two teeth had left his mouth. The third and fourth slams definitely showed me that he was going to have a hard time chewing anything ever again. The fifth and sixth slams were a reminder to myself that I wasn't playing games. I pulled his head back to see his face so I could assess the damage. It was beautiful. His face was completely busted up and I wasn't even sure if he was alive. I holstered my gun and grabbed my knife to finished the job. A quick slice to the throat would suffice but if he was alive I wanted him to suffer. I stabbed him in the hand that was still attached to his worthless body and he flinched. The man was still alive so I pushed his face to the table and rubbed it as he rubbed mine to distraught my breathing. The only difference was he was in greater pain than I was when he did it.

He shouted as much as he could through all the blood as I kept rubbing with no remorse. I took my knife and drove it into his back multiple times quickly, over and over and over again. I screamed, as a form of release of the anxiety that I had held in my body, until the son of a bitch was nothing more than a bag of meat.

I left the knife stuck in him as I made my way over to the kitchen where I found a pail with water that I could use to clean myself off. The good thing about leather was that blood didn't stick if you applied water, and that's exactly what I did. When I was finished cleaning myself off, I went back over to the dead body and pulled out my blade. I stepped back to the kitchen to wash off the blood on the knife.

I felt good. I had finally begun to avenge Evelyn and for the first time since all this started I was beginning to feel alive again. I was about to walk out of the kitchen when the prostitute came into the apartment with someone. I couldn't tell who it was as I pulled back and hid myself.

They didn't say a word as they just walked around and inspected everything. I could hear more than two people walking around, I figured she had grabbed her pimp to come stop the conflict. I grabbed a couple of bullets from my jacket pocket. I unholstered my Colt and put the bullets into the empty slots. I closed my baby up and kept it ready for action.

As I hid in the dark corner of the kitchen I could see someone going over to the bed and grabbing the guard's belongings. When I peeked, I saw Conor. What the hell was he doing here? I stayed hidden and waited until they all left the apartment.

I quickly exited the apartment and ran towards the back hallway window. I opened it and leaped down onto the alley. The good thing about New York was all the alleys that could make for quick getaways.

CHAPTER 11: MASTERMIND

I walked towards the Refinery with my focus directly on killing Vlad. I stopped a few feet back from the entrance and gulped on some water I had put into a jar at the apartment, until my thirst was quenched. Unless someone had done it themselves, you wouldn't believe how thirsty you could get from beating a man's face into a table.

I could hear the sound of chariots approaching; gunshots were the easiest way to get the cops called for a disturbance.

I ran down the street and passed by the apartment I had just been inside of and turned the corner. A dozen cops, together with Detective Murphy have rushed up into the apartment.

If it was any other circumstance, I'm sure I would of heard someone creep up beside me, but all my attention was on the cops. I suddenly felt a nudge on my back.

I quickly shot over to see Vlad's other guard towering over me. As I stood there frozen not understanding what was happening, I didn't move. As he reached out his hand, he revealed a pipe. My eyes followed the pipe continuously until everything went dark.

I awoke in the middle of the street. It was very dark in the night. All the snow was gone but deep down inside I felt cold. Suddenly I heard a trash can fall in a nearby alley. I could see Vlad, his two guards, Detective Murphy, his assistant Annie, and everyone I had killed all looking at me in disgust. I ran down the road as fast as I could looking back constantly to see if I had lost them.

As I looked forward, there stood a yellow door right in the middle of the street. The door had no walls around it. The door clearly made no sense but I wasn't ready to ask questions as I needed an escape. I opened the door and rushed inside.

There in front of me lay Evelyn on a couch in her sleeping wear. Her hair was up just the way I liked it. She looked stunning as always, and I was ready to make love to her. Evelyn rose to her feet and met me half way. I grabbed her and we began to kiss passionately. As I took her to the couch, she began to take my shirt off.

As I lay over her, we continued to kiss. My eyes were closed as I was enjoying the moment until my mouth began to give off a weird taste— the taste of blood. I opened my eyes and saw Evelyn laying in a pool of blood. The couch was gone and we were back in the apartment. That's when I remembered everything that had happened. This was all a dream.

I awoke to the smell of shit. I opened my eyes and waited to adjust to the light that was in my face. As my eyes settled, I opened them wide and looked down to see myself tied to a chair. Hell, Vlad's goon had knocked me out cold. I wasn't psychic— I could feel my head pounding over my left temple.

As I studied my surroundings, I could tell I was definitely in the Refinery. The darkness outside showed me it was late out. I had been knocked out at least a few hours.

The door ahead of me opened and there, no more than five feet in front of me, stood Vlad.

I tensed every muscle in my body as I attempted to break free. "Ahhhhhh I'm going to kill you!" I shouted angrily, while foaming at the mouth.

"Calm this dog," Vlad ordered as the huge guard came up to me and back handed me across the face.

What power the man had as I thought my mouth had cracked in half. I wiggled my jaw from side to side to set it in place.

The two men I wanted to kill, no— I needed to kill were right in front of me. I was helpless to do nothing about it again, just like I was helpless to protect Evelyn.

"I knew you would come. It was only a matter of time," Vlad said mockingly.

I again tried to free myself from the chair but it was no good. The bear of a man towered over me once more and punched me in the stomach with his chariot sized hand. The air was knocked straight out of me.

"Did you know that I answer to higher ups? Yes.. I'm telling you this because I want you to know. There is no way in hell you're walking out of this Refinery alive."

"You're not the loan shark?" I asked confusingly.

"No, I'm just the middle man, the hired muscle."

"So who ordered my wife's death? Who's the loan shark?" I asked attentively, waiting for his answer. I would still kill these two but if there was another behind all this he too would die.

"Don't you worry, you sack of piss. You don't get all the answers. What you do get though is a nice present."

I was confused as I watched Vlad signal his man to do something. The big ogre made his way out the door as I could hear him shuffling something. I could hear someone moaning as he brought in Father Edwards, who was tied and gagged.

Vlad got up in a hurry and pushed Father onto the chair right in front of me. "You see, you're helpless again, and the only other person you care about is going to die. You're destined to be alone."

"No, I don't care for this man," I blurted out, which was clearly a lie. This man was the closest thing to a father that I had. I was just trying to keep him alive.

"I don't believe you. Father, do you have any last words?" Vlad asked as he took the gag out of the Father's mouth.

"Son, don't give into the snares of the devil. These things are only happening to you as a test from God," Father Edwards said to me.

"Oh, enough. I don't have time for this stupid talk," Vlad said as he gagged the father again.

By some miracle, I happened to slip my hand free and pull my other hand loose while Vlad and his friend were occupied with preparing their plan.

I looked over and saw my knife and the Colt Navy pistol lying on a table. I quietly rose to my feet and grabbed the knife, throwing it at Vlad. It grazed his arm as he looked at me with fear. Noticing me reaching for the Colt, he ran out of the room.

It was just me and the ogre of a man, who was now charging at me just like the time at the apartment. The only difference was I had a gun. I pointed at his leg and shot his knee cap clean off. His leg buckled under his weight and he dropped to the ground like a sack of potatoes.

I stood over the huge man as he seemed so small beneath me. The man caught me unexpectedly as he hooked my legs from right under me and I dropped to the ground. He tried to reach for me but I squirmed my way free. I ran and grabbed the pipe he had knocked me out with and hit him over the head with it. The big man was taking a nap.

I grabbed some rope that they had used on me and tied his arms and feet together in the form of a hog tie. I wanted to make this man suffer even more than the last so I looked around the room again in search of a good idea. Then I came up with one, and this idea had me really excited. I stepped out of the room and found a bucket. I grabbed it and then looked as I saw a few rats near a cage. I grabbed three rats and placed them in the bucket. I went back into the room and turned the bucket onto the stomach of the man as he lay flat on his back. I grabbed one of the candles and pointed the fire to the bucket.

"Don't do this, Lawrence," Father Edwards shouted.

"Father, I must do this for Evelyn."

"This is not justice."

"What do you know about justice?" I said as I looked away. Father didn't say another word. We just waited in the silent room.

After a few moments, the rats began to move. The heat from the candle would cause immense heat inside the bucket, which in turn would cause the rats to flee to survive. The only way through would be the flesh of the man. The huge man began to wake up but it was too late. The rats began clawing their way through him as he spat blood from his mouth violently. You could see in his face the immeasurable pain he was in as his voice was silent. The pain was so much that he couldn't even find his voice. As the man died, I watched in excitement. I now needed to find Vlad and figure out who the true mastermind was.

I grabbed my knife from the corner of the room and untied Father Edwards. I put the knife back in my jacket. I was going to ask if Father was alright. But as I turned, there he was, the man of God pointing my own gun right at me.

"Father, what are you doing?" I asked in confusion and sarcasm.

"You're the devil" Father Edwards said very upset.

"I know you're afraid but put the gun down. We both know you won't shoot me. Just walk away and I'll forget this happened. I just need to finish this," I explained.

"I would be a fool to let you leave from here," the Father said as he cocked the gun back.

"Easy Father, think about what you're doing," I said as I tried to reason with him.

"I have thought about it," As Father said those words, the room echoed loudly into the silent night sky—BAM! BAM! Father had actually shot me. I could feel myself becoming faint as I looked down at my body and noticed two bullet wounds in the chest. There was blood seeping like a faucet. I grabbed my chest as I felt a rising burning sensation and then a piercing pain that sent shivers down my spine. I collapsed to the ground and could see Father Edwards fleeing. As I began to lose consciousness, I didn't regret what I had done, only that I would never be able to avenge my sweet, sweet Evelyn. I lost consciousness and my world became silent like the night.

CHAPTER 12: FOURTH OF JULY

I awoke in a void of darkness that surrounded me. I couldn't make out my surroundings, hear anything, or even see my own feet. "Hello?" I shouted but to my surprise there was no echo, and no response. Where the heck was I? Was I dead? I reached my hands ahead of me fully extended as I began to creep slowly through the darkness. I carefully placed each of my steps firmly before releasing the weight off of my other foot. "Hello!" I practically screamed. I was feeling claustrophobic now as the darkness was ensnaring me in its powerful grip.

What seemed like forever was nothing more than five well placed steps, as I was reluctant to just step anywhere. I had a constant fear that I would step into a hole and fall endlessly. Ahead of me, I could see a very faint light flashing. It almost seemed to want to grab my attention. The little flicker in the darkness gave me a sudden sense of hope and I no longer feared the darkness or holes in the ground. I began to run to the light, hoping to feel the warm embrace of its gaze hitting my skin.

When I arrived at the light, it had a diameter of four by four feet. I stood right in the center of it and noticed a floating lamp. It was odd but I wasn't in a place for debate. The floating lamp was the only way I could see myself as I looked down and noticed my clothes were not dirty with my blood and the blood of others.

"There you are. I've been searching forever for you." A voice came from the darkness— Evelyn's voice.

I quickly spun around as she emerged from the shadows. She too was alright.

"Evelyn!" I belted as I grabbed her and we kissed.

"Where are we?" Evelyn asked as we both looked around.

"I have no idea, but I think we're dead."

"You died?" she asked confused.

"Yes, Father Edwards shot me."

"He practically raised you when you were younger." Evelyn then added, "What have you done since my death?"

"I have been searching for justice," I responded softly, honestly ashamed of what I had done. My anger had brought me to such rage that I would kill a person with no remorse. But now that I was in the presence of Evelyn, I felt ashamed.

"I told you not to blame yourself," she insisted as I could hear a bit of disappointment in her voice.

"I know but my rage made me kill people." I thought Evelyn would be upset but she just smiled. It was creepy, and she didn't seem right— something was off about her.

"Why did you let me die?" she asked with a terrifying smile across her face.

"I tried to protect you but I was too weak," I explained as I began to tear.

Evelyn smacked me across the face. My face throbbed as I grabbed my cheek and looked at her puzzled.

"You're pathetic. You're a weak human being that couldn't even save his wife from a couple of thieves."

"What do you mean? You told me to not blame myself," I added in confusion.

"You will always be weak," Evelyn said as her voice echoed into the darkness and she stepped away from the light. She then added in a huge voice that seemed to fill the entire dark voice, "AND ALONE."

The lamp above me exploded, as the glass shattered all around me. "I'm sorry," I said in a faint whisper.

I could hear firecrackers in the distance but everything was dark. My God, was I in the same shit storm again? I opened my eyes and saw myself in a beautifully designed room. I lifted my head off of the mattress I was lying on and saw I was actually laying on a bed. This seemed very real and I was not dreaming. I attempted to lift myself from the bed but a sudden pain sprang me back into the lying position. I looked over to the window and could see the flickers of firecrackers in the sky. The echoes of each explosion of a light show brought confusion to my thoughts.

I observed the room again and could tell I was in a very elegant room that had to be in the uptown region of New York. I looked over at my night stand and instantly felt relieved to see my good friend lying there. The long barreled Colt Model 1851 Navy pistol rested comfortably at my side. I reached for it with my right hand and went with my left to open the gun and see how many rounds I had but my arm didn't move. I looked down and used the barrel of the gun to pull my sheets off my body. I was bandaged where I was shot and my left arm was lifeless. I realized my arm was paralyzed from the gunshot.

The door knob on the door began to turn and I quickly cocked the gun back and pointed my pistol to see who would enter. The door opened and in came Grace Murphy, the gun shop owner.

"Grace?" I asked in confusion as I lay the pistol down at my side on the bed.

She smiled and ran back for the door. "Gregory he's awake!" she shouted in joy as she turned and came to my side. She planted a big hard kiss of excitement right on my forehead and then sat at the chair next to me. She seemed different, her hair was longer, and her appearance wasn't the same as the last time I had been with her at the gun shop, the day I was given the pistol.

"Who the hell's Gregory?" I shot out as I looked at the door waiting to see this man.

"We have a lot of catching up to do, you and I. You should just be thankful you're alive."

"How did you find me?" I asked as I kept looking at the door.

"I had been with my father one day and overheard him talking with one of the other officers about the murder in the apartment. The victim had been shot by none other than the gun you had and his face was beaten severely. I knew it was you and started retracing your steps."

"So detective work runs in the family?" I asked rhetorically.

Grace smiled as she ran her fingers through her hair and sat forward on her chair. Her face then went pale. " I watched you kill that man with the rats."

I looked down at the mattress. I didn't want to talk about the things I did, the things I had to do.

"Most people would call you a monster," she insisted. "But not me. Love is a powerful force and when someone gets their ties of love severed... What I want to say is I understand why you did it."

I didn't say a word as I felt I had no reason to explain myself. "How long have I been asleep?" I asked.

"I don't know exactly but I would say four months."

"Four months! There has to be some sort of mistake here."

"I assure you it's not a mistake. You weren't sleeping; you were in a coma. When you were shot it was the middle of February. If you haven't noticed the firecrackers, it's the Fourth of July."

I was shocked as I looked down at my body. She must have been telling the truth. I looked scrawnier than I had been. Now that I knew months had passed, I could see the difference in my body. I looked over at my shoulder, "My arm, it's paralyzed."

"Yes ,your shoulder was severely damaged and you had to go under surgery from my friend, Gregory. He saved your life, but he couldn't save your arm," she explained as she looked at my shoulder with a look of distress.

"It's alright, I don't need my arm. I'm done," I said calmly. The dream had to have been a message for me. I was being traumatized by weird dreams and I needed to stop this dark path.

"Done?" she asked confused.

"I'm done with the path of vengeance. I have a second chance at life," I answered. I had no desire to kill anyone. The dream I had felt like a message from Evelyn, for she would be unhappy if I killed in her name. I had lost my self emotionally but now I seemed rejuvenated.

Gregory walked in wiping his hands on a cloth like he had just been washing them.

"My apologies for taking some time to come upstairs," he said as he came around to my side just behind Grace. He stuck his hand out. "My name is Gregory Timmons. I have been looking after you to nurse you back to health. How are you feeling?"

I stuck my arm out and shook his hand. "Thank you, and I'm alright," I said sincerely.

The well-groomed man smiled in return as he came around to the other side of the bed now. "If I may, I would like to just check the wound?" he asked with his hands hovering over me, Waiting for my permission."

I nodded and he lifted the bandage. "If it's been four months then how could I still have a wound?" I inquired.

Gregory examined the wounds while softly answering, "I have had to go into surgery a few times in an attempt to save your arm."

"Ouch," I said as the bandage was attached to my scab.

"If you may; turn on your right side. Grace, please help Lawrence," Gregory requested. Grace stood up from her chair and grabbed my side gently, helping me lay on my right side.

Gregory removed the bandages and then further examined the wounds. He slid his chair back a notch and reached into a cupboard. I looked over my shoulder to see what he was reaching for.

It wasn't a gun or a knife like my subconscious was telling me. It was a fresh bandage and ointment. It made no sense why I would think such a foolish thing. If they wanted me dead there was plenty of chance to execute when I was in a coma.

"You both know who I am and what I've done. Why do you help me?"

Gregory answered first. "I don't care what you have done, I owed Grace a favor and she called in that favor with you. I studied human biology and then worked side by side with physicians so she knew my expertise would be useful in this situation."

Grace added her opinion in the matter. "I am attracted to you and I don't know why but I care for you and your whole situation."

"Your father is looking for me and you're here playing house?" I asked.

Grace cut in. "My father has moved on. The commissioners of state have forced him to take himself off the case. No one is looking for you anymore."

That was a sense of relief to hear. A huge weight had been lifted off my shoulders.

"I want you to confess to me how many people you have killed," Grace insisted in her voice

"Why must I talk about that? I would like to leave it in the past."

"If you admit your faults to someone, it will make you feel better, believe me. Dad has worked closely with psychologists and confessions help the mind ease itself from mental trauma."

I looked down at the mattress again as Gregory guided me back and helped prop me up into a sitting position.

"I have killed seven people," I said bluntly.

"Who? Names?" Grace insisted.

It almost seemed like she was too interested in knowing the details. I knew there was the possibility of her working with her father and needed a confession to pin the murders on me but I almost didn't seem to care. I just wanted peace in my life so I said the names. " Ben Johnson, my landlord, your fathers assistant, Annie Wilson and the two officers that were with her in my pursuit in the catacombs, and the loan shark's two guards that held me down during the murder. Also, a street thug, a real piece of garbage I..."

Grace cut in, "strangled him in the ravine"

"Yes, wait now I remember. Vlad mentioned he was the hired muscle." My memories were coming back to me.

"I needed to talk to you about that," Grace said faintly.

"Why? Do you know who he was working for?" I asked

"I don't know who, but I know someone who is in the same trouble you were in with owing money to Vlad."

"Who?" I shot forward with desperation in my voice.

"Joseph Baker. He has been seen around the Refinery lately."

I lay back against the backrest of the bed and took a deep breathe. "The fool," I mumbled as I looked out into the night sky. I didn't care much about him but I wanted to help him for Evelyn's sake. After that I would leave New York City for good. He found Vlad for me and now he too had asked him for money? Maybe for Evelyn's funeral costs? It was an honorable thing to do for Evelyn's memory, taking care of her family. But I also needed to remember Joseph would probably kill me when he saw me. It was a risk I was willing to take for my conscious.

"Who does your father say to the press murdered my wife. I'm still the prime suspect right?" I asked.

"Yes, he ignored the story you told him."

"Of course he did," I shot back.

"I say we let the man get some sleep," Gregory explained as he walked out to the door.

"I agree," Grace added as she reached in and kissed my cheek.

She stopped inches from my mouth and our eyes locked. My wife had died four months before. I felt awful for feeling what I was feeling at that moment, but I was attracted to this woman. Grace opened her mouth slightly and invited my tongue in as I kissed her with great emphasis. She pushed me off as she walked away to the door. I was confused but didn't say anything.

I thought she would leave but she closed the door and turned to me. She began taking her clothes off and though I was weak, I could feel energy surging through me. I got up off the bed slowly and waited until she was naked to grab her and lay her down. We had sex that night and I felt what I had longed for since Evelyn's death. I felt love.

CHAPTER 13: PROTECTION

The next morning I awoke with the sun hitting my face. I tried to get up without waking up Grace but she moved and opened her eye slightly towards me. "Where are you going?" she asked.

"Going to the John," I responded as she rolled over and revealed her long beautiful leg and gorgeous soft hip. I felt excited for her again as I grinned and put my pants on. I felt safe in the home with Grace and Gregory but I still reached and grabbed my Colt from the night table, I walked out of the room and down the steps. I went outside and placed the gun by the window ledge while I urinated on Gregory's flower bed. I guess that was my thanks for him saving my life. He would quickly end my life if he saw me killing his flowers.

I looked down at my useless arm and realized life was going to be a lot more difficult without two arms. It took me an extra moment to adjust my pants but I finally worked them back comfortably on my waist with my one arm. I grabbed the gun off the window and looked around.

"Nice quiet neighborhood, ain't it?" Gregory asked as he perched himself on the wooden veranda railing of his home, overlooking the side of the house where I stood.

"It's very nice," I responded as I looked around, trying to play off what I had done.

"You won't need your pistol here, son."

"I appreciate the confidence but my friend, 'Colt' here, goes where I go," I declared.

"Fair enough. At least grab your holster so you can free your working arm. I'll make you breakfast in the meantime. How does that sound?"

As I looked out towards the city beneath me, I nodded and then looked back at Gregory. "I like how that sounds."

"Great, I'll start on the breakfast then."

Gregory was making his way back inside when I walked over to the front of the house and called out to him "Gregory?"

"Yes," he replied looking back at me.

"I need to get to the Five Points. Can you help me?"

Gregory looked stunned. "Today?" he asked with utter shock drawn all over his face.

"Yes of course. I have been out quite a while and I have matters I need to attend to."

Gregory, through a sarcastic laugh, almost like a belt of air shot straight from his lungs in a form of a hiccup, "Don't be absurd you need bed rest for at least another couple of weeks."

I nodded and turned my back on him overlooking the city again. I could hear the door closing behind me as he went inside to make breakfast. My body was shaking with exhaustion and every muscle was tighter than a virgin, but I pondered how long did Joseph have to live until Vlad decided to 'collect'. Joseph had no lover so Vlad would attack Susan and John. The thought of those good people dying sent an uncomfortable feeling into my stomach. I had to get down to the Five Points and find him before it was too late.

I walked back into the house and made my way upstairs. I could smell what seemed like bacon and eggs being made in the kitchen down the left side of the long hall. The hall was vast and had about five rooms on each side and a study at the end directly adjacent from the front door. The hall upstairs was no different— what an enormous house for one man. I walked into the bedroom and placed my gun on the chair. I reached my hand out and awoke Grace slowly.

She opened her eyes slightly and rubbed them with her palms to clear the water from her eyelids. She looked at me and rose from the bed naked giving me a cheerful kiss.

I looked around and found my holster lying with my jacket on a table by the door. There was a fresh, new white shirt neatly folded on the side of the jacket, and my boots were polished anew under the table. I approached the table and grabbed the holster, applying it to my pants. I turned around to grab the Colt but Grace was already bringing it to me as she slid the pistol into the holster pocket and reached in giving me another kiss.

"I'll help you get dressed," Grace offered as she grabbed her clothes and dressed herself quickly. I leaned against the table as I waited for her, feeling exhaustion.

"So how did you sleep?" she asked me while putting her dress on.

"I slept ok," I responded, watching her get dressed.

"That's great to hear. So listen, I was thinking we get out of New York and start a new life together." Her cheeks blushed at the comment as she grabbed her top turning her back to hide the embarrassment of rejection.

"What are we doing here?" I asked with emphasis.

She looked back at me "We are moving on with our lives."

I took a big gulp and looked down at the floor. "I feel guilty that I am not avenging my wife, but it feels like a long time ago. Me, nearly dying has changed my thoughts on the matter. Who am I to serve justice, when I am becoming even worse of a human than the men I hunt."

Grace now fully dressed came to me. "What is it that you want to do?" she asked me sincerely as she grabbed my hands. I could only feel her human contact on my right arm. My left was like dead weight being a thorn in my side.

"I need to explain myself to my in laws and help her foolish brother. Only then can I leave this place."

"Alright, when you're ready we will head down and tie loose ends. I do have a question," she said as she let go of my hands and pulled her hair back to tie it up. "How are you going to get the money to pay off Joseph's debt?"

I watched her tie her hair up, which brought back memories of how Evelyn would tie it the same way.

"Lawrence?" she asked confused watching me space out.

I snapped out of it. "Sorry," I apologized. "I will have to do one more illegal action."

"No way, you're not killing anyone for money."

"I'm not saying anything about killing, more like robbing."

"Why don't you find out how much he owes and then we will work out a plan with him." Grace stated as she reached for the folded shirt on the table.

"We also will have a problem with that. He thinks I killed his sister. I hate to ask you this but I need you to approach him for me and ask how much he owes."

"You think he's just going to tell me how much he owes? That's absurd," she proclaimed as she put my shirt on for me.

"We don't have a choice, Grace. It's all I can think of. Besides, I'll be watching you from a safe distance."

"That's reassuring," she said with a playful hint in her voice as she helped me into my boots.

"Oh, come on," I replied with sarcasm in my voice. We laughed aloud as she grabbed my jacket and walked to the door.

I grabbed her by the arm and swung her closely towards me. "I will never let anyone hurt you," I said as I kissed her.

"I know, Lawrence," she agreed as she looked me in the eyes and turned walking out into the hallway.

I followed as we walked down the long corridor. I felt so confused at how I could have feelings for a new woman when I was on the darkest path one could take just the last time I had been awake. Somehow the time I had been in the coma changed me, settled my mind. I was now afraid to die.

Grace and I made our way downstairs and into the kitchen where the breakfast was ready on the table. Gregory was already seated.

"Hey, you two. I thought the breakfast was going to get cold by the time you came down."

"I apologize, Gregory. It is not a simple task to dress with one arm."

"Nonsense. I was just messing with you," Gregory replied with a snaring grin. He got up from his chair and slid our chairs back as we both sat at the table. He joined us and I looked down at the food.

I couldn't remember the last time I had eaten, long before even the coma.

"I must ask, how did I not starve to death while in the coma?" I inquired.

Grace and Gregory shot a look at each other and both giggled.

"What?.. What's so funny?" I asked in confusion.

"I put a tube down your throat to your stomach and you ate mashed food," Gregory explained.

"What about the bathroom?" I asked with a hint of disgust in my voice.

Gregory looked over at Grace while chewing on his food, and spoke with his mouth full. "She changed the diapers."

I looked at Grace in awe. She really did care for me deeply to do such a thing for a stranger. I didn't know why. "Thank you, I am forever indebted to you."

"Not at all, Lawrence," she replied, placing her hand on mine then continuing, "I care for you ever since I saw you the first time at my store."

That reminded me. If she was here then what happened to her store? "What about your store?" I asked as I took a bite of the egg

"There were riots on the street when the people discovered you were missing. People blamed the police department for their failure to do their job. Knowing well I'm the lead detectives' daughter, people burned the building to the ground."

"What?" I asked in awe. Without even realizing it at all, I had affected so many people's lives with my quest for retribution. "I'm so sorry," I apologized as I looked at her with deep regret.

"It's alright, everything happens for a reason. The state gave me five hundred dollars for insurance money. I've decided that if you want to leave with me, we could use this money to start a life."

I was beginning to feel almost as though she had overthought this too much. How could she even be attracted to a murderer like me?

"How long has the trail been cold in finding me?" I asked as I began to eat the bacon.

"One month. You have been listed as a wanted serial killer with a murder rate of eight people, including your wife, and some man, Tom Finagin that you didn't mention yesterday," Gregory explained.

"I didn't kill Tom Finagin either," I answered sharply.

"You're an open case that has been now passed down to the surrounding states," Grace added.

"If they find you now you won't even get a trial. You will instantly be hung to death," Gregory shot the awful truth at me like a smack across the face.

I finished my food and leaned back against my chair. I killed and killed without any remorse not thinking of the consequences of my actions and now I felt such a burden of what I had done. It didn't make any sense. I had started killing for vengeance, then even killing a man for the sheer enjoyment of it, and now was it all just gone? The urge to murder had just vanished.

"They won't find me. I will be in and out and I will never be discovered. If they couldn't catch me when they were looking for me, they definitely won't catch me now," I assured them both.

Gregory grabbed his plate and took it to his sink to wash. He returned and grabbed Grace's and then looked at me. "You all done?" he asked.

"Yes, thank you," I responded as I rose from my seat. Grace sprang up from her chair and smiled at me with a naughty smirk.

I smiled in return and then proceeded out the kitchen into the hallway, making my way to the front door again. Grace accompanied me and grabbed me by the arm. I looked back at her and asked, "what's the matter?"

"Gregory has friends, friends that can get us into Five Points with security."

"Has he offered you those friends?" I asked as I rubbed an itch from my nose.

"I'm working on it," she grinned as she kissed her index and middle fingers and then pressed them against my lips. Her index finger pushed down on my bottom lips and she turned away swaying, giving me a naughty look. I watched her walk away. I had feelings for her— I could feel it in my knees. I wanted to move on and leave everything in New York behind me. I had to stay a few weeks to recover completely but fleeing without helping the Bakers would tarnish the memory of Evelyn. I couldn't do that, not for her sake. I needed to do this, I needed to talk to her parents, save her loser of a brother, and visit her at the gravesite one last time before I would leave; never to return.

I made my way outside and sat on the front porch. Grace came outside and stood above me.

"Here, I got this splint to hold your dead arm up so it's not in your way," she said, lifting my arm and tying the splint to the back of my neck and around my arm, holding it up in a bent position.

"I've been thinking. Could Gregory just chop it off?" I asked looking down at the nuisance of a limb.

Grace's eyes widened. "Are you mad? Why would you want to amputate your arm?"

"It's just in the way," I stated as I looked down at it again.

"Lawrence," she said as she reached in. "Just leave it, ok?"

"Alright, it was just an idea," I said.

She reached in and kissed me again. I grabbed her and sat her on my lap.

She wrapped her arms around me and pressed her face near mine as we looked down towards the city.

"I really hate that we have to go back down there," Grace exclaimed. "But since we are going, I would like to make another stop and say goodbye to my father."

"You think that's a good idea?" I asked. I shouldn't have; he was her only family. Why wouldn't she want to say her goodbyes. She would definitely never see him again.

"I have to, Lawrence. Me and dad were never close but he's my father. I just want the closure."

"I understand," I replied. "Gregory says I need to rest for at least another couple of weeks. Would you just want to go in the meantime and say goodbye to him?"

"That's actually a great idea. I'll head down tomorrow morning and be back by the afternoon." Grace put her lips close to my ear, whispering, "I was going to talk to Gregory but I wanted to give you the splint first. Let's go see what he says then?"

"Let's try," I replied as we both made our way inside.

"Gregory!" Grace shouted but there was no response. She called again as we made our way to the kitchen. "Gregory!"

"I'm in the back," shouted a faint voice through the kitchen window.

We walked through the kitchen and out the back door to his backyard. Gregory was collecting some water from a well he had out by his stable.

As Grace and I walked towards him, she said, "He worked with my dad by the way. That's how I know him."

I looked at her and nodded. That caught me off guard. He was a cop, and he was actually aiding a fugitive. That was very interesting.

"What is it sweetie?" Gregory asked as he placed a full bucket of water to the side and grabbed another empty one. He tied the rope to the handle of the pail and dropped it into the well.

"I need you to call your friends," Grace said but was cut off quickly by Gregory.

"Not a chance. That's not going to happen. I'm done with them."

"You know they would come and help if you asked," Grace insisted.

"Who are his friends?" I tried to ask but they ignored me and kept speaking.

"I don't ever want to get involved with those people again."

"Please, I'm begging you. They would be the best way of keeping Lawrence hidden," Grace insisted again.

"I told you it's not going to happen!" Gregory now shouted as he reached in for the rope, pulling the pail out of the well.

Grace spun around in a fury and ran for the stable. I was going to go after her but Gregory raised his hand to stop me.

"Listen kid, me and her dad weren't always on the right side of the law. When we were younger, we were part of a gang named The Bowery Boys and well, we lost close friends and almost our freedom. So we left."

"They just let you leave?" I asked since there were rumors how once you joined one of the gangs down at the Five Points you could never leave again.

"I never officially left. I just took a high paying job and gave them a cut— but Owen left. They chased him and tried to kill him on more than one occasion. To protect himself from them, he joined the police department," Gregory explained.

"Now Grace is asking you to get help from them," I stated rhetorically.

"Yes, and it's not going to happen. They're not good people. They would kill you and collect the bounty on your head instead of aiding us. She doesn't know them like me and Owen do."

Grace came out of the stable on a horse. "I'm going to go see daddy now," she said as she waved at me.

"Alright, be safe," I shouted as she rode the horse off the property. I hated having her leave but there was no way I was prepared to go downtown just yet.

CHAPTER 14: SAME SITUATION

Most of the day had passed and dusk was beginning to set in. I was feeling a bit worried as I didn't expect Grace to take this long down in the city. I sipped my ale from a cup and then chugged it right down to the last drop. As I placed the mug on the front porch, I heard a chariot approaching. I ran inside without hesitation and Gregory met me at the door.

"Get inside," he ordered as he exited the door. I watched from the front window, peeking through the curtain as a chariot pulled up by the front door.

The chariot door sprung open and Detective Owen Murphy jumped out of the cabin coming towards Gregory in a hurry.

"Owen, now what do I owe the pleasure?" Gregory asked with open arms.

"Some thug, Vlad, has my daughter and wants money for her. He's saying she will be the exchange for the money Lawrence Talbot the serial killer never gave. He's blaming me saying since I never captured him it's my fault."

"That's awful," Gregory said as he put his hands on his face.

"That's not the worst part. I know Grace was very fond of that monster but I received a little message saying you have a guest here in your home. That's one hell of a coincidence that Grace was up here too and I never saw Lawrence again," the detective said as he looked at the house over Gregory's shoulder.

"That's absurd. Why would I hide a worthless fugitive in my home. My uncle was here until yesterday because we hadn't seen each other in a long time."

The detective looked back and signaled his hand calling more officers as they exited the cabin. "Then it won't be a problem if I search your residence."

"Owen," Gregory shouted, but the detective made his way to the porch and climbed the two steps looking down at the mug I had left on the porch. The detective grabbed the cup and smelled the substance as he looked back at Gregory. He threw the mug at his feet.

"Arrest this man, until further notice," the detective ordered as Gregory tried to fight himself off. But the two officers grabbed him and pushed him to the ground, arresting him.

"You come with me," the detective ordered to the third officer as they both unholstered their pistols and made their way to the door.

I was trapped by the window as I slowly hid behind the couch. My jacket was upstairs and if they saw it then it would be all over for Gregory. I needed to escape without showing my face. It was the least I could do for the man who saved my life. It was time to return the favor.

The detective walked down the hallway into one of the farther rooms, as the officer went upstairs. I peeked up and noticed the coast was clear as I walked to the end of the room and looked out the front door. The two officers were walking Gregory to the chariot and so I looked back over to the hallway. The coast was clear so I slowly made my way up the steps trying to not make a sound.

The officer was making his way to the last door on the right. I needed to get to the last door on the left, so I waited. I could hear footsteps making their way down the hallway towards me and I was forced to keep moving forward. The officer stepped into the room and so I kept sneaking my way by until I crept into my room. I closed the door slowly and grabbed my jacket throwing it over my shoulders. It hung over my back like a pirate captain would wear it back in the fifteenth century. I made my way to the window and opened it.

It was a minimum of a six feet drop. I hesitated as I looked back at the door hearing steps approaching. The doorknob to the room began to turn and the door swung open. I no longer needed any reason to stay and so I jumped out the window crashing hard into the rose bush I had urinated on that morning. Like I said earlier, what you do in life comes back around to bite you in the ass. I pissed on the man's flowers and now I was lying on my own urine.

I lay in the bushes cursing at myself for jumping as my body ached everywhere. I looked over at my shoulder and noticed my wound was bleeding. I was supposed to be resting for a couple of weeks and instead I was jumping out of windows and playing ninja.

The door to the backyard opened and my eyes widened in fear as the light from the candles in the kitchen illuminated the backyard a bit now that the sky was dark. I rolled over slowly as I unholstered my pistol and cocked it. I didn't want to kill any more people but if I had to then I would. There was no way I could die before saving Grace. I would not let history repeat itself again. Losing another woman I cared about to the same man would not happen. I would even kill her own father just to assure my safety out of here.

The detective walked around looking for evidence but didn't find any. I didn't move a muscle the entire time while he scoped the area. I think at times I forgot to even breathe. The detective then walked towards me. I lifted my pistol right at him just waiting for him to make his move. He stopped directly in front of me and turned facing the backyard. The barrel of my pistol was pointed right up his ass, and I was just waiting for a reason to make him a new hole. The detective thankfully gave me no reason and he walked to the front of the house.

I crawled out of the flowers and made my way to the side of the house overlooking the front yard. I watched as they took the cuffs off of Gregory and let him go. He walked back to his home as the detective and his officers made their way back into the chariot. The rider whipped the horses and the chariot shot down the road back into the city.

As soon as the coast was clear, I ran out into the open and approached Gregory.

"Thank you for that Gregory. I am forever in your debt."

"You don't need to thank me, Lawrence," Gregory said as he patted me on the back. "We do, on the other hand, have to go and save Grace."

I nodded in agreement. "I'm ready when you are," I stated.

"Meet me in the back by the stables," Gregory said as he climbed up the porch and went into his home.

I walked around the side of the house and made my way to the stables. I stepped inside and noticed an enormous box unit covered in a cloth. I heard steps approaching and immediately looked back to see Gregory walk in.

"That's going to be our ride into town," he said as he pulled the cover off the box revealing his chariot.

Gregory quickly set his two remaining horses to the front of the chariot and opened the door. "Get in," he insisted.

I stepped into the chariot and he shut the door behind me. He climbed into the rider's chair and we began to move out of the stable.

I reached forward through a small crack where the rider and people sitting inside of the carriage could communicate. "What's the plan?" I asked.

"Plan? We will go down to the Five Points and find this Vlad. If he doesn't give Grace up, then we're going to have to get our hands dirty one last time."

I didn't want to kill again but I knew Gregory was right.

I sat back in my chair and looked out the window. I knew what was coming as Vlad would never hand Grace over without a fight. I would have to kill again, even if I didn't want to. My stomach turned at the thought of losing Grace. I would not lose her, no matter what had to be done.

CHAPTER 15: FORGIVENESS

We rode down the streets of New York in the late hours of the night. I watched through the little window, which was nothing more than a square cut out of the wood, separating the outside world with the inside of the carriage by four steel bars. I watched as we passed the church in which Father Edwards resided.

"Gregory, stop," I practically ordered as I opened the door and hopped out of the carriage as it still rode on the street.

"What is it?" Gregory asked as he yanked on the horses and stopped the carriage dead in its tracks.

"I need to pay an old friend a visit, here at the church."

"At this time of the night? Wouldn't the priest be sleeping?" Gregory asked but knew I would go in anyway. He was already jumping off the carriage and grabbing the ropes of his horse to tie them to a street pole.

"This priest is the person who shot me," I stated with no emotion as I kept my eyes on the church.

"Alright, just give me a minute," Gregory said as he finished tying the horses and walking calmly to my side. "So what's our next move? You leaving a trail of dead bodies again?"

"No," I cut in immediately. "He will live beyond this night if he does exactly what I say," I stated as I began walking to the entrance of the church.

I knocked on the front door using the huge steel rings that were bolted to the door for that purpose. The loud consecutive thumps of steel banging against the wooden doors echoed throughout the neighborhood. Gregory looked around hoping not to attract attention.

"You think he..." I pressed my index finger against his lip to shut him up as the door began to unlock.

Father Edwards opened the door still rubbing his swollen eyes as he held a candle to illuminate his path through the dark church. He looked up at me, eyes widened as if he had seen a ghost.

"Good to see you again, Father," I said with a menacing grin.

Father Edwards turned back attempting to run into the church but I grabbed him by the collar as I entered. I tossed him against the wall and then held him, while the entire time he managed to hold the candle upright. Gregory checked the streets and then entered the church as he closed the door behind us.

"Father, this is Gregory. Gregory, this is Father Edwards. Now I'm going to let you go but don't try anything and you might live through the night."

Father Edwards, in utter fear, nodded his head in agreement and I released him from my clutches.

"Take me and my friend here to your quarters," I demanded. Father didn't put up an argument at all as he began to lead the way. I could tell in his posture that he was very scared for his life. Honestly, I would be too if I thought I had killed someone but they were here living, and breathing in front of me.

We entered his room and as we made ourselves at home, Father Edwards lit more candles to illuminate the room well.

"Lawrence, I was afraid. You have to believe me," Father tried to explain.

I totally ignored his apology. "How does a priest live with such a secret weighing down his soul? Murdering a person in cold blood? You had the gun, Father. You could have just handed me to the authorities. But no, instead you killed me and then obviously regretted it as you didn't tell the officials that I was dead. So now I'm nothing more than a phantom.

"If you're not going to kill me then what do you want?"

"Do you believe there's a spot in Heaven for you now?" I asked as I ignored him again. I could tell he was becoming frustrated but his fear for his life was greater so he kept his mouth shut.

Gregory watched us by the door as he kept his hand hovering over his holstered pistol in case the priest got confident.

I pulled my jacket off my shoulders and let it fall back into the chair. I rose to my feet and approached Father. "You paralyzed my arm. Now you will pay for killing a part of me."

"Please don't hurt me," Father Edwards wept and begged as he covered himself from me as if I was a hideous beast. I burst into laughter and Gregory giggled but I could tell he also was confused.

"I mean literally pay me in money."

Father Edwards showed his face again slowly as he looked at me. "Just money?" he asked.

"What else do you think I want? Your virginity?!" I belted.

Father stiffened straight in shock. I must have looked damn scary because I could see Gregory also shoot back from my comment.

"How much do you have in your safe?" I asked as I pointed at his bed. I knew his safe was under his bed as he had kept it there for years.

"I have one hundred fifty dollars," Father responded in a quivering voice

"That will suffice as payment. I will forgive you for what you did to me, Father," I said and I really meant it.

Father reached under his bed and grabbed the little safe as he slid it out into the open. He reached for a key that was tied to a necklace around his neck, under his clothing, and unlocked the safe. He collected the money and handed it to me in a bag. I grabbed the bag and handed it to Gregory as he counted the money on the table. Father closed his safe, slid it back under his bed and then stood before me.

I reached my hand out in the form of a hug and waited. Father hesitated but then gave in and gave me a frightened hug. I squeezed him close and then said, "I understand, Father, and I forgive you now. You were my closest friend. Take care of yourself." I let go of the father and grabbed my jacket. I gave him a slight smirk as Gregory and I walked out into the open mass area.

"Wait a minute," Father shouted from his quarters.

Gregory and I both looked back to see Father coming to meet us.

"Will I ever see you again, Lawrence?" Father asked me as his eyes sparkled from the candles in the distance.

"No, I will be like the phantoms of the dark and disappear into distant memory," I responded.

"Take care of yourself, Lawrence."

"I shall, Father," I replied.

Gregory made his way to the door and shouted back at me. "We must keep going."

I waved my hand showing Gregory that I agreed and looked back at the priest one last time.

"Though your sins are like scarlet, they shall be white as snow; though they are red like crimson, they shall become like wool." As I finished saying my verse, I turned around and walked outside the church meeting Gregory who was standing by the carriage.

"I was certain you were going to kill him," Gregory said.

"I would like to never take a life again. I figured I would get the money from him and pay for Grace's freedom," I stated. I knew this would be a long shot but I had no other choice.

"Good evening fellas" a dark-skinned woman said in a fair voice as she approached us.

I turned around quickly and put my hand on my revolver. "What's the matter whore? We aren't interested," I said as I waved her off and turned around again.

"A man of God shouldn't rob the church of its funds," she answered immediately.

How could she know of that? Gregory and I both unholstered our pistols and aimed it at the woman.

"Easy boys. I am a friend," she muttered as she grinned. "I just know things, that's all. I would like to make you an offer," the mysterious woman said as she pointed her index finger at me, drawing my body out as she winked from one eye.

"What do you want then?" Gregory asked still holding the gun out towards her.

"You give me all the money you collected from the church and well... I'll give you your arm back."

I laughed hard from deep in my belly as that was impossible. I looked up almost expecting the woman to be joining me in laughing but she was not— she was dead serious. I stopped laughing instantly and looked back at Gregory. His eyes met mine and his face was pale as snow.

"What's the matter with you? You not feeling well?" I asked.

"I don't do well with witchcraft. This stuff scares the daylights out of me."

"No one mentioned any witchcraft," I replied as I looked at the lady. Gregory had seen what I failed to miss. The lady held in one hand a knife, and in the other hand a little baggy. It had symbols on it which meant it had to be none other than a hex bag.

"You want your arm back or not?" she asked calmly.

I approached her and looked her dead in the eyes as I holstered my gun, "Give me my arm back and you got yourself a deal," I answered confidently. I was being foolish. I didn't even believe in witchcraft and it was more just to show Gregory that witches were just frauds trying to make a living.

"Give me your arm," the woman commanded as she waited with her hand extended to grab it. I reached over and allowed her to pull my arm forward as she made a tiny slit in the arm sleeve of my shirt. She then looked at me and then looked at my arm as she began chanting some words under her breathe. I looked back at Gregory and then felt a pressure against my arm. I looked forward at my arm and noticed she had stabbed me with the knife.

My arm was dead and it was no surprise I couldn't feel it but it still came as a shock to me. She released the knife and put her fingers against the flesh of my arm and widened the hole. I watched in horror at what seemed like a bad dream. She used her other hand to insert the hex bag and then stepped back and smiled. I watched her step back slowly smiling like some lunatic at my arm. I felt a cold chill rush through my arm which was accompanied by an intense burning sensation. It was extremely painful but I could not find the words to scream.

I looked down at my arm in horror and then noticed my fingers were all bent in different directions. I shot a glare at the woman. "What have you done to me?" I yelled as I looked back down at my hand. My fingers were normal again and all the pain had subsided.

"Make a fist," the woman said calmly.

I did as she said and I couldn't believe my eyes. My arm was moving! I looked up at the woman again and now she had a serious face and just watched me. I might have killed many people but this woman gave even me the creeps.

"Gregory, throw me the purse," I ordered as I held my now working arm out.

Gregory tossed the purse towards me and I caught it. I lightly tossed the purse towards the woman as I didn't want to get too close to her. She caught the purse in mid-flight and then smiled at me.

"One hundred fifty dollars," she stated as she looked at the purse and walked away.

I walked back to Gregory and we didn't exchange a single word. Gregory prepared the horses while I sat back inside the carriage staring at my arm.

CHAPTER 16: INNER DEMONS

After waking up from the coma yesterday, I never thought in a million years I would come back to the Five Points. But here I was. Gregory and I slept inside the carriage until dawn crept in. The roosters sang, which had awoken us from our slumber. I'm sure that if the roosters had slept in this morning, I too would have joined them as over sleeping in a coma was even more exhausting then physical labor. Gregory and I sat in the carriage silently for a while. We never spoke of the witchcraft that had happened last night. I could tell Gregory had a real fear for that kind of stuff like people have fear for spiders, or tight spaces.

"The last time I came down here, Vlad, who has Grace, was at the Refinery," I informed Gregory.

"Then that's where we will go," Gregory responded as he reached under his seat and lifted the secret compartment. He grabbed two big knives and handed me one while he placed the other one across his belt. I too liked the idea and ran my blade across my belt. Gregory reached for the handle of the carriage door and swung it wide open. He stepped outside stretching his legs and I soon followed.

We walked casually down the road to not arouse any suspicion even though there were no more than a handful of citizens walking the streets this early in the morning.

"Now that we don't have the money, what are we going to do?" Gregory asked as we made our way down the first street.

"Whatever has to be done. I would prefer no bloodshed but this Vlad character won't go down without a fight. I killed a few of his friends so I'm sure he will be glad to see me," I stated sarcastically.

"Well then I'm glad that I brought my weapons," Gregory said as he giggled.

"I'm just glad to have both my arms again," I said, hoping to spark a conversation about what happened yesterday. It was no good; Gregory didn't answer anything to my comment.

As we reached an intersection no more than two blocks away from the Refinery, a pair of officers met us as they stared at us from head to toe. I looked down at my shoes and pretended to clean a speck of dirt from my boot to avoid eye contact.

To my surprise, what I was hoping to avoid actually happened anyway. One of the officers spoke. "Good morning, gentlemen. Where are you both headed to this morning?" the officer asked as he wiped the sweat running from his forehead.

I froze in fear as I prayed not to be recognized but Gregory responded for me. "Just heading down to the Refinery is all."

"The Refinery? Well what business you fellas got going down there?" the officer asked curiously. It was really none of their business but cops always had the sense of a power trip. They wore the uniform which meant they were untouchable. This was clearly was false since I had three dead cops under my body count. They obviously didn't need to know that.

I looked up at them as I finished cleaning my already spotless boots. "We're just looking for jobs," I answered coldly.

"Your friend here giving me lip?" the officer asked with hostility in his voice as he looked at Gregory.

"No, he just has no manners," Gregory said as he looked back at me widening his eyes hinting me to stop talking.

"Just saying we're looking for jobs. How is that giving you lip?" I asked rhetorically. I didn't want to kill anyone, but being down in the Five Points was making my dormant evil want to surface.

The officers both pulled out their batons and began to approach me.

Gregory jumped in the midst of the cops. "Please officers, no need for this. I'll set my friend here straight. I know you officers are busy, Just go on and do your duty and I'll whip this here fool into shape for you," Gregory assured them.

I grinned at the officers as they began to walk away. I wanted to stop but I felt as though my control was slipping once more. Something about this city was bad for me. I needed to get out, and the sooner I left the better. All I needed was Grace and I would never return to this nightmare of a city. I loved this city once. It was my home all my life. But too much had happened here now and my soul was tainted when I stood on these grounds.

I honestly didn't even want to even deal with the Bakers anymore. Dealing with Vlad would clear Joseph's debt and then that was it, I would leave.

Gregory walked back to me and grabbed me by the shirt, shoving me against the window of the shop behind us.

"Don't you ever do that again, you hear me?" Gregory demanded with explosive anger in his eyes.

I grinned at him but didn't say a word. I imagined shooting both those officers in the head, and the thought gave me such pleasure. I was glad I had just thought about it and had not actually gone through with the action.

"Now keep your shit together and let's go," Gregory said as he crossed the street.

I adjusted my shirt and jacket and followed him.

We walked the next couple of blocks without exchanging any words until we reached the Refinery. "There it is," I said as I pointed straight ahead.

Gregory took a deep breath and then began to walk to the main entrance. As I walked alongside my new companion, I looked over to the left and saw the apartment that I had killed the pig that was going to sleep with the hooker. I reminisced on the smashing of his face against the table. Each time his face made contact with the table, I could remember it. I could still feel it. The vibration and sounds of cracking skull. It was exhilarating.

I snapped out of my trance and realized I was standing in the middle of the road alone. I looked ahead and noticed Gregory had made it to the front door and began to make his way inside. I sprinted to catch up to him and when I did we both looked around. To my surprise, the Refinery was much different now. It was clean, and empty. We searched around every room and every area but there was nobody here.

We stepped back outside after sometime and leaned against the wall.

"Where the hell did this snake go now?" Gregory asked as he reached into his pants pocket and pulled out a cigar.

"You smoke? Since when?" I asked in confusion. I had never seen Gregory smoke or even smell the stench on his clothes while I was at his home.

"I don't smoke," he responded with anger in his voice. He was still pissed off at me, I could tell.

"Then why do you have a cigar in your hand?" I asked. I didn't give a crap if he smoked or not but I was just trying to make conversation to lighten up the mood.

Gregory put the cigar to his lips and pulled on it as he lit it with a match. He blew the smoke outwards and gave a subtle cough. "I quit smoking when I quit crime," he replied.

I knew what he meant by that. I knew it too well. It was almost the same thing that had happened to me with the officer's just moments ago. Coming back to our roots was causing our inner demons to surface. Mine was a spree killing lunatic, his was a smoker. Both were a vice that would harm us and get us killed if we didn't stop.

"We just got to find some rats," I said as I looked around hoping to find a thug walking by. There was no one. The streets seemed much cleaner than usual.

I began to walk down the road as I put my hands in my pants pocket. Gregory followed me as he kept smoking his cigar. I reached the alley where I had chased the thug to the ravine. "Garbage used to hang out here so I'm going to check it out for a rat," I said.

"We stick together," Gregory responded bluntly.

I walked down the alley with Gregory. We looked around to see if we could find someone that could lead us to Vlad. The alleyway too was empty. Either even the street thugs had places to live, or the police department was really cracking down on petty crime. We eventually made it to the steps that I had kicked the thug down. That's when I noticed a thug hanging down by the ravine. There was some serious nostalgia at that moment seeing another thug by the ravine.

I walked down the steps and looked back at Gregory. "Stay here and watch the alley," I said as I continued walking.

"Alright, be quick," he said as he blew smoke from his nose.

I made my way down to the ravine and stood next to the sleeping thug. The thug woke up alarmed and tried to flee. I ran after him and tripped him to the ground.

"Easy fellow, just need you to give me some information," I said.

The thug screamed and tried to fight me off.

"Shut up," I demanded as I tried to cover his mouth with my hand.

The thug continued to scream and I knew I had to shut him up. I also knew I was curious to see if my arm was weaker than the other, so I clenched my left fist and hammered the thug's mouth. The thug moaned in pain as blood rushed from his lips.

"Now shut up or next I'll gut you," I said as I stared the thug down.

"Ok, what do you want," he said as he wiped the blood from his mouth.

"This could have been a lot easier if you had just listened," I explained as I got up from lying over him. "Where is the loan shark, Vlad, hiding out these days?" I asked.

"Vlad...Vlad, I don't know no Vlad," he said as he wiped the blood from his mouth again.

"You don't know Vlad, eh? Well I know something that will jot your memory," I said as I pulled out the Colt and put the barrel in the man's mouth. He gagged on the barrel and tried to squirm free but I wiggled the barrel around as he grimaced in pain. I pulled the barrel out but kept it two inches from his forehead. "Anything coming to memory now?" I asked rhetorically as I knew any person with a bit of a brain would spill the beans at this point.

"Yes, please. He's under the protection of the Forty Thieves," the thug said as he looked at me

I stood there speechless. How could that snake be hiding behind one of the strongest gangs in New York. This was about to become a lot worse now.

I made my way up the stairs and met with Gregory who was perched over a fence. I too perched over next to him. "We have a big problem" I said as I looked ahead of me down the underpass of the ravine.

"What's the problem?" Gregory asked as he shot a stare at me.

"Vlad's under the protection of the Forty Thieves. There's only one way we could get close now."

Gregory cut me off. "No way, Lawrence. I told you already, there's no way I'm going back to ask those guys for help."

"If you don't get The Bowery Boys to help us then you can kiss Grace goodbye. Her death will be on you," I said as I pointed my finger stiffly into Gregory's chest.

"You have really put us into a shit storm now," Gregory said as he turned his back to me.

"Don't blame it on me. You're the one who upset her to the point that she ran away."

"You son of a bitch," Gregory screamed as he turned to me and punched me in the face. The blow caught me off guard as I stumbled to the ground. Gregory ran towards me to pounce on top of me but I kicked my leg across his path and tripped him to the ground. I got up on my feet, and he too met me half way. He tackled me hard as I stumbled back, holding him. We both tumbled down the long steps towards the ravine.

'What comes around goes around' had proven itself once again. I had kicked the thug I murdered down these steps just some odd months ago and now I was the one being sent down them. We both lay in a considerable amount of pain. I looked over at Gregory and noticed him lighting another cigar still lying down. He looked at me also and we began to laugh.

"This is really going to get complicated from this point forward. I hope you understand that."

"I do understand, and personally, I wish I could just run away and never come back. But we need to do this for Grace," I explained as I laid my head back against the ground and looked up at the sky.

Gregory got back to his feet and reached his arm out to me. I grabbed his hand with mine and he helped me back to my feet. We dusted ourselves off and climbed the steps. At the top of the steps, Gregory pulled on the cigar hard and then blew the smoke through his nose again.

"Alright, Lawrence, let's go to the Bowery and talk to Roy King, the leader of The Bowery Boys."

CHAPTER 17: OLD WOUNDS

When I was a kid, I remember my dad used to get drunk very often with his friends. I also remember one night when my great and noble father passed out on the couch and his friend, Charles, took advantage of my mother. The first time was painful to hear, but by the hundredth time I'm sure my mom had given up caring and went along with it, so I no longer would lose sleep. What made it worse was that when my father passed away from a heart attack, my mother started letting Charles stay over to apparently 'help her around the house'—Yeah right, more like help her not stay lonely.

Rape is a very sensitive thing to me when I hear or see any of it. I don't tolerate it at all. My mother stayed with the bastard until they both passed away, but I knew she was miserable when he first started raping her.

There was also a boy at school that went by the name of James Miller. James was a good kid. He had good grades and was always the one child that when the teacher asked any question he would raise his hand straight in the air and wave it back and forth. "Mrs, Mrs.," he would practically beg for the opportunity to speak. It was freaking annoying. Well one day, I don't know what happened to him but he lost his mind. The most beautiful girl in our school, Sara Huntington, was going home from school under the underpass by the ravine, the same place where I strangled the thug a few months back. As she walked under the underpass, James stepped out in front of her.

James didn't know I was a few feet behind and when I saw them talking I hid behind the wooden frame of the underpass.

"Hi there Sara, umm... well... you're so beautiful," James said as he had his hands in his pocket and looked down at the floor, blushing.

"Thanks," Sara said as she started walking by James.

"Hey, why do you got to be so rude for?" James asked clearly upset.

"I'm sorry James, but there's someone else," she said as she walked away. I could see that James was shattered as he sat by the underpass for a good twenty minutes. I needed to pee so bad and that was my only way home, but I waited patiently because I didn't want to have the awkward moment of passing him. After quite some time, he left and I was finally able to go home and tinkle.

The next day was when it got bad. Same as every other day, we went to school, James fought to answer every question like his life depended on it, and Sara was naturally beautiful.

After school, I saw Sara going home and James stalking her from a distance. I knew that wasn't a good sign so I hung back a safe distance from James and stalked the stalker.

When Sara reached the underpass, James ran for his prey. Sara turned around startled to hear the approaching footsteps. She tried to fight the big boned boy off of her but she couldn't. Being teenagers, we were definitely flushing with hormones, but what James did to poor Sara was wrong.

I stood a safe distance away and just sat flat on my ass with my head tucked between my knees hearing this poor girl getting raped. I was too chicken to go and save her.

I never had the courage to tell James what I saw that day, and what made it all worse was when Sara didn't show up to school for two weeks.

I overheard her mother speaking with our teacher and saying something like, "she's cut up bad" or "raped." She must have been all cut up inside by that dog. Over the course of the next two weeks, she probably appeared at school twice until that one morning.

I will never forget it. These are the defining moments that change a person forever. My teacher came to the front of the class and cleared her throat. I can see her rolling her eyes as if she's trying to find the best way to say something awful.

"Kids, well Sara was very ill lately, and she passed away last night."

I looked back at James as he sat there with that smug face. I think that was the first time I really wanted to kill someone. I later found out she had committed suicide by grabbing a kitchen knife and slitting her wrists, apparently down to the bone.

There were so many days that I followed James home with my own kitchen knife hidden under my jacket. I wanted to summon the courage to gut the son of a bitch but I never found it. I would daydream all day of how I would do it, and roll over at night every time I had failed.

Then the school year was over and James moved out west. I never saw him again.

My mother being raped was awful, but Sara would haunt me forever. I hoped for many years, every single day, that James had died a horrible death and if it wasn't too much to beg to God, if he could die of dick cancer or something. Puss spewing out, having him wear diapers until the last day that miserable prick lived.

For some reason, Gregory wanted to know what I had done to the first of Vlad's guards as we walked by the apartment. I explained it to him with such joy. He definitely didn't find it as fascinating as I did as his face scrunched often when I described the smashing of his face to the table. I went on and on for a good five minutes but was interrupted by what sounded like pots and pans slamming to the ground. I looked up in the direction of one of the apartments and asked "Did you hear that?"

"I sure did— maybe it's nothing," Gregory responded as he too looked up at the window. The window was old and the wooden frame was detaching from the brick. The winters would definitely do that as the snow would melt and turn to slush, rotting the wood. Every other year you would see the construction workers busy as usual. If you were in the construction field then you had work all year round. Eight dollars a day and one meal on the job was a dream job to any regular folks. If Gregory and I hung out here for the next week I'm sure we would see them coming to fix this window. One week from now I wanted this city to be nothing but a distant memory.

A scream tore through the open window. I was already beginning to walk away and Gregory had relaxed his stiff shoulders. We both looked at each other and agreed to run upstairs.

We ran up to the floor and waited with our ears facing the hallway to spot the disturbance. We approached the doors of the hallway slowly and noticed one room had feet shifting around often. Who would be moving so much this early in the morning?

"Stop! Ahh, your hurting me!" a woman's voice shouted from one of the rooms. My heart stopped but Gregory gave me no time as he reacted almost instantly as he kicked the door in.

I could hear Gregory unholstering his pistol as I ran in behind him. What got me by complete surprise was the man that was butt naked with his pants around his ankles, forcing himself on this woman, who was face down and butt up in the air. It was none other than my brother-in-law Joseph.

I ran to him in a rage and grabbed him by the shirt. I practically dragged him over to the wall. I looked down at his thin legs, which were spread apart to hold his pants from falling lower than his knees.

"It's cold out in July, isn't it?" I said as I giggled over to Gregory, who was helping the lady to the other room. I could hear her thanking him a million times until she shut the door to the other room.

"Get off me, you piece of shit," Joseph said, practically spitting in my face upset.

"I'm the piece of shit? When you're the one who's so desperate for pussy that you're raping a woman," I stated as I got in his face.

"She's just a cunt, a nobody," Joseph insinuated as he reached down and pulled his pants up in a flurry.

I remembered Sara. I backhanded Joseph clean across the face, which made him stumble into a nice lamp the woman had in the corner of her apartment.

"You motherfu..." His anger fell short to the face of my barrel, which was ready to splat his brains all over the back wall and probably damage the lady's beautiful lamp with his brain juice.

"I don't need to justify myself to you, you worthless shit. But know this. I loved your sister and I did what I had to do to survive, to get revenge for her."

"I always knew you were no good for her," he replied, collecting himself from the blow he received.

Gregory stepped over and punched Joseph square in the mouth. I looked at him confused as he came from nowhere with that one.

"You know this fuck?" Gregory asked as he rubbed his knuckles.

"Unfortunately," I replied as I rubbed my hand down my face, feeling the stubble of beard growing in. For the first time since this nightmare started I didn't know what to do with someone. To kill him would be awful for the Bakers. They had already lost one child and they would definitely be destroyed with their only child gone. Spare him and he would probably rape again. I couldn't have another Sara on my conscious.

"Where's your boyfriend, Conor?" I asked Joseph with a smirk.

"Conor got clipped last month."

"Oh that's too bad. I would have enjoyed it more if he was here," I said with God honest truth. I really did wish that Conor was here— I would have killed him to send Joseph a message.

I lowered my Colt as I stepped to the window to gather my thoughts.

"You blame yourself for her death don't you?" Joseph asked as he got up to his feet.

Still looking out the window, I replied calmly. "Everyday."

"Who else's fault would it be?" he asked rhetorically with a smug grin on his face. I noticed it as soon as I looked at him. I also noticed Gregory reaching in and pistol whipping Joseph right back down to the ground. "Shut up," Gregory demanded as he stayed right over Joseph, who was holding his head as though it was about to fall off. A pistol whip will cause a tremendous amount of pain if hit right over the temple. Hell, it would really hurt just about anywhere.

As I stood over the window looking at Joseph, I could hear horses approaching. I shot a quick look down at the road to see Detective Murphy and two dozen officers running out of there carriages.

"There he is!" shouted the detective with a huge smile of excitement. I'm sure he was excited as this would be his chance to catch me. The time for games was over. I was caught and had to fight, and not just run again.

I ran back into the room and closed the door to the hallway.

"Joseph, hold this door back. Gregory help me get this table over to the door," I demanded and neither of them did anything except exactly what I had ordered.

Joseph held the door back as the thumping began, while me and Gregory grabbed the heavy table and slid it to the door. Joseph held the door back with all his might as he struggled. The table came fast and Joseph fortunately for his abdomen ducked right under the table in the perfect time to slide right from underneath us.

"Watch out next time!" Joseph screamed.

"What the hell are we going to do now?" Gregory asked.

"Who gives a shit? I'm leaving," Joseph said as he made a break for the back window.

I wanted to stop him but I didn't— I let him jump out the back and then took a few steps to the window and looked back at Gregory.

"Greg… over here" I stated pointing at the window for him to jump through first. I liked Greg instead of Gregory. It had more of a ring to it and personally I just had dry mouth which caused that fluke to sound good. The cops bust the door in as Greg had made his jump through the window, and I had just dodged a bullet on my way down as I followed.

As I collected myself from the drop I noticed Greg had his gun pointed at a cop, who held Joseph by the throat from behind. Gregory was clearly contemplating what to do but I did not hesitate. I pulled my gun out and shot the cop clean between the eyes. The bullet must have zoomed by Joseph's face as he looked back in shock at the dead corpse that collapsed at his feet. The bullet hit as close as two inches away from Joseph. One slip and he would be the corpse not the officer.

I could hear screaming and panting from the upstairs room as I looked at Joseph. "You're on your own," I explained. As I ran off, I could hear Greg behind me. I happened to look back down the street to see Joseph fleeing in the other direction. He was probably running to his gang for support. I couldn't believe I was actually thinking this but I was envious he had somewhere safe to run. Now that I had been seen at the apartment, there would be a state wide manhunt for me again, and this good man, Greg, would be caught in the cross fire just like Evelyn and Grace. Speaking of Grace, I hoped she was hanging in there. I was coming for her soon.

CHAPTER 18: BARGAIN

Gregory and I ran down the street as quickly as we could while never looking back. Every chance that we got we took full advantage of the opportunity to get more distance from our pursuers, as we weaved in and out of the crowds of people now flooding the streets to shoot the shit or buy food at the stands. The officers weren't playing anymore, they had their guns drawn so being in the line of sight was a good way of getting ourselves killed.

We hugged the wall and made a quick right turn between two apartment complexes, which led downhill into a ditch.

"Down here!" I shouted while I simultaneously pointed and jumped down, letting gravity do its work. Let me tell you, gravity definitely did it's work as I bumped and scraped my way down the entire time. We landed hard down at the bottom of the ditch and collected ourselves almost instantly as we sprang to our feet and gunned for the next street over.

We could hear people shouting from far behind us but we didn't look back to see if it was the police. We had enough evidence to know it was them as bullets flew by us dangerously close. One time a bullet flew right between my legs and shot a speck of dirt a foot high as I kicked it while running through it.

We prayed, pushed forward and thankfully escaped unharmed. We blocked ourselves against the two apartment complexes that were very close together. I was on one end and Gregory was on the other as we both looked down the alley back to where the ditch was. I could see cops rolling down the ditch and I'm sure they were sending more around to flank us.

"Greg, listen. I just remembered we need to get back to Joseph," I proclaimed.

"Did you hit your head or something? If you haven't noticed yet, back is where the cops are running towards us," he replied exhausted and panting his voice as he collected himself while spitting the sticky phlegm from his throat.

Gregory had a point but I needed Joseph so I explained. "Joseph can lead us to Vlad, and Vlad can lead us to Grace."

"That's all you needed to say then. Why don't we go around?" Gregory asked as he pointed in the direction behind me. I looked over my shoulder and noticed the road was clear and a straight run around. Hopefully the cops were flanking us from the other side and we would escape unharmed. I was nervous and my heart was beating violently against my chest. I couldn't understand if it was nerves, excitement, or just fear of getting killed, or worse— caught.

I ran down the street where Greg had pointed too, and he began to follow. We now jogged, attempting to catch our breathe again while repeatedly looking back to see when the officers would come out into the street.

We ran one block, then two, then three so we stopped for a second to plan our next move.

"Je...sus" Gregory said panting in exhaustion as he wiped the sweating beating from his forehead.

I stood up firmly with my hands resting, one on each side of my hips. I looked down the road as I licked my chapped lips. I was thirsty, exhausted, and tired of freaking running. Everything I didn't want to happen actually happened, and now the search and rescue of Grace was going to be near impossible. At this point, the only thing making me push forward was to know who truly planned Evelyn's death, and I didn't want to lose another partner again. Hell I didn't want to— but more so I couldn't handle that pain once more.

We had stopped for a good minute not exchanging words. Words used up energy, and we were in short supply of it. We didn't want to exhaust any that we didn't have to at the moment.

A carriage burst down the street as officers pointed towards us. I swear to God Detective Murphy is the most persistent son of a bitch I had ever met. He led the charge standing atop the carriage resting his weight on one knee. I'm sure it wasn't because he was exhausted. It was more so to balance himself on the moving carriage to avoid flying off.

"Give up!" Detective Murphy shouted but I was having none of that. I ran with all my might into the art museum.

Luckily, there were hundreds of people in the gallery, which was a three-story building. As we rushed in, I looked around for a quick escape and found the long staircase towards the back right corner of the grand room.

"Greg, over here," I said, waving Gregory over. He rushed without thought and we made our way to the steps as composed as we could to avoid suspicion. The detective burst into the room with three officers at his side as he raised his gun in the air. I watched in horror with Gregory from the upstairs balcony as we knelt and crept through the beautifully white, crafted wooden railing.

Detective Murphy was red to the face like a tomato as he took deep breathes of air into his lungs before screaming, "everyone get the fuck out!" As the Detective shouted the orders, he took his pistol, aimed it to the ceiling and let out two shots, which sent everyone in the museum into a panic.

"Lawrence, we need to get to the roof. There's nowhere to go but up," Gregory said as he looked at me still holding the railing for dear life.

I looked over at him and could see his fists clenched tight to the railing as if he was being drifted away by a powerful current and the railings were his only lifeline. The man was scared shitless and I knew he was right. "Alright, let's go quietly, and keep low," I whispered as we crawled into the next room.

The screaming of people was almost deafening. If the room wasn't any bigger I'm sure my ears would have bled. We kept moving, making sure to never stay still to avoid detection. Detective Murphy was a calm and highly intelligent person. I'm sure that's where Grace got her qualities from. But I could see the man had changed. Owen, and yes I'm calling him by his first name—was out for blood, out for vengeance. I had killed Annie, three of his officers, and disappeared into the night, all without him touching me.

Gregory was the first to storm out the roof door. He kept his momentum going as he ran across the roof until he came to a sudden halt looking around frantically. I rushed off to the left and looked out. I realized why Greg had stopped— there was nowhere to go.

"Lawrence, Jesus we're screwed," Gregory belted at me as he grabbed my shirt, panicking.

"Calm down," I insisted but Greg was beginning to lose his mind with fear.

"Do you know what's going to happen to me when Owen sees me up here? I can't get hung for this man, I can't."

I could hear the footsteps of the officers rushing up the steps and I reacted as quickly as I could. I grabbed Greg's gun and hit the butt of the pistol right to his forehead. I tossed the pistol aside and drew my gun while wrapping my arm around his throat, facing us both to the door. I kept his body in front of mine to conceal most of my body from getting shot before I could speak.

I whispered into Greg's ear. "Play along," I said as I pressed the gun against Greg's temple.

The detective and the three officers ran out onto the roof and all pointed their guns towards us while spreading out.

"Easy, Lawrence. Don't add more bloodshed on your hands." The detective said. I could tell he was nervous as I was sure he didn't want to lose his friend. I would have to use that to my advantage.

"I will not kill this man, who has been following me for quite some time. He believed I didn't notice him until I got the chance up here," I said while jabbing him with the barrel of the gun against his head. Greg shouted loudly which I could tell was so fake. But he made it sound authentic to people who weren't in on our plan.

"What do you want then? Tell me Lawrence," The detective said with sincerity in his voice.

"I want you all to drop your guns and kick them towards me," I demanded.

Detective Murphy hesitated but I helped make up his mind. I flailed Gregory around like a rag doll and then shouted, "I'm not going to ask again."

"Alright men, drop your guns and do as he says," The detective ordered as all four of them dropped their guns and kicked them over to my direction slightly. The guns were nowhere near me but they were also a few feet away from them, which put me in control of the situation. Control was what I liked the most.

"I'm going to call you Owen if that's alright."

"Sure that's fine. Tell me what's next," Owen said as he stood firmly waiting for my next words.

"During my time of hiding and searching for my targets, I have come to discover that your daughter is being held prisoner by the Forty Thieves."

"I know that already," Owen said as he exhaled loudly and looked to the ground.

"What are you going to do about that?" I asked.

"What the hell does it matter to you, a psychopath, what happens to my daughter and what I'm going to do about it?"

"There is actually much that matters to me about the well-being of some. She presents a problem because I don't want to harm her when I kill my next target, who so happens to be with the thieves at this very moment."

"So her captor, he isn't part of the gang? He's just nested with them?" The Detective asked with raised eyebrows.

Bingo. I smiled big showing my satisfaction at his expression. He hid the smile as soon as he was on to me. "You didn't know that did you? Now you will let me go and you will bargain with the Thieves to let Grace go and give up Vlad Reznik."

Owen looked at his officers breathing heavily. "Let this man go. He had aided us in retrieving my daughter."

"Sir, there is nothing more important than the capture of this man," one of the younger officers argued.

Owen looked at him with hellish eyes. "You speak a word of this to anyone at the department and I will personally cut your balls off, you understand?"

"Yes, sir," the young officer shouted. He was no more than twenty, a decent looking man with a clean shaven face which made him look even younger, so young that he was probably straight out of the academy.

"I'm going to get my gun," Owen said as he reached for it cautiously— but I didn't move.

"Go, and I will let your friend leave unharmed. You have my word."

"Why are you helping me?" Owen asked before leaving with confusion in his face.

"Don't be mistaken Owen. I am not helping you. I am helping Grace because I owed her one, Tell her the debt is paid for getting me out of the jam when we first met at her store."

Owen smiled and nodded, running down the steps of the museum and out of sight. The officers all looked at me and then grabbed their guns and holstered them before running down the steps also.

When the coast was clear I released Greg and holstered my pistol.

"That was some good thinking, Lawrence," Greg said as he rubbed his temple. "A little too good if you ask me."

"I didn't ask you," I said while smiling.

"You cocky prick," Greg said while walking to the other side of the building. He looked back over to me and screamed, "so now what?"

"Now we wait until Vlad is captured and Grace is safe. You will leave with Grace, and I will break into the police department and kill Vlad once and for all."

Greg's eyes almost shot clear from their sockets while giving a disgusted look. "You really have some loose screws up in there man," he argued as he pointed at his head with great enthusiasm, imitating that I was mentally disabled.

CHAPTER 19: SENDING A MESSAGE

I knew that I wasn't out of the woods yet but in the meantime I could collect my thoughts and find a good place to hide while Vlad was being taken into custody. We kept to the crowds to avoid being seen by officers but as the hours went by we noticed there weren't any police on the streets. It was late afternoon when we made it to the Five Points. There were officers everywhere and in clusters questioning people.

Gregory and I made our way to a group of civilians. "What's going on here?" I asked hoping to get some information on Vlad and Grace's status.

An old lady looked at me. " The detectives daughter has been released but her captor has fled just minutes ago after a standoff. It was very scary."

I looked over at Greg, who took a deep breath of relief at Grace's freedom.

"Thank you," I said to the old woman as I bowed and began to walk away.

Gregory followed. "So this Vlad character has to be close by."

"Yes that's for sure. With these many officers around and him releasing Grace just minutes ago I'm sure he is very close. I wonder how the detective got the Thieves to give up Vlad?" I asked while scratching my head.

"Should we attempt to ask one of the Thieves if they know where he has gone?" Gregory asked me while already looking around to find one.

"I guess that could be our next step," I agreed as we stopped and turned back towards the Points.

We stayed nearby as we stalked the Thieves who were sitting outside in a group just shooting the shit as usual. A part of me wanted to just pull out my Colt and kill them all for dragging Joseph into that lifestyle, but he was a man and could make his own decisions. I guess I still held on to Evelyn's feelings, which was understandable. All the days I had to comfort her because she would always worry that every time Joseph said goodbye that was the last time she would see him alive. She feared discovering he had been killed and tossed by a dumpster like a piece of trash.

"Greg, when one of them veers off you grab him and I'll do the work,?" I said hoping for agreement.

"You got it," Gregory replied as he pulled out a cigar and lit it.

We waited and waited and seemed to have died of boredom until finally one of them veered off from the group. It was perfect timing to grab the thief as dusk was falling over us and the cops were beginning to disperse. Gregory was looking in the other direction while puffing the smoke of his cigar into the air as I tapped his shoulder. He swung around to see me approaching the thief and he quickly joined.

I loved the Five Points for my attacks because of all the back alleys and many possible exits you could use in case things got hairy. I was getting very irritated and so 'hairy' was definitely going to happen. I was killing Vlad today no matter the cost.

The thief turned into one of the apartment complexes and we stayed a way's back, making sure to be unnoticed but close enough to run up on him when the time was right.

The thief opened the door and as we were about to exit our cover, uproar from the Five Points erupted. I turned my shoulder in confusion at what could be happening to cause such a stir. My vendetta would be put on hold as me and Gregory began to run back to discover what was happening. In seconds, there were crowds and crowds of people huddled all around in an enormous circle. I pushed and shoved through the crowds to get to the middle and see what had happened. I peered over the last person that was standing in my way and I noticed someone lying on the ground.

I shoved the man aside and he practically just glided as he let me through. I couldn't believe what I was seeing, Father Edwards was practically naked, wearing only a rag like underwear and he had words carved into the flesh of his chest.

"Father!" I shouted as I reached down to grab him. Father was already dead for quite a while. I could feel his cold skin against mine and the wounds on his chest were already drying up. I held him but pulled myself back slightly to read what the wound said. Greg peered over me and looked on. 'Phantom's next'.

I lay my old friend down and got up in a fit of rage running through the crowd into an alleyway before the cops arrived. I felt an emotion I had not felt since Evelyn's death. It was sadness, I could feel the tears streaming down my face as I tried to wipe them before Gregory could see them. I felt him put his hand on my shoulder and caress me while I crouched down to the ground. I was so upset at Father Edward's death. He shot me but I forgave him because he was like a father to me.

"We will get that asshole, don't you worry," Gregory assured me as he patted me on the back.

I needed to stop him. He killed Evelyn, captured Grace and now sent me a message by killing the priest. He was trying to take everything from me, and now I knew I couldn't stop until he was found.

"I don't expect you to go any further with me in this Greg," I said as I got up to my feet.

"What do you mean?"

"Grace is safe, and you came along with me so we could get her back."

Greg looked at me with a fire in his eyes. "Listen kid, this is bigger than just saving Grace now. Were friends and I can tell you're not the monster the world is making you seem. You're actually a victim in all this and you must have really loved your wife to turn to darkness like you did for revenge. This is a crazy ride and I'm in it to make sure you survive it so you can run off into the sunset with Grace. She will be fine. She's in protective custody now."

I placed my hand on his shoulder and grinned. "Thank you, Gregory. I'm forever in your debt."

Gregory nodded at me and replied, "Don't you worry about it."

CHAPTER 20: AT LONG LAST

The night was young and the moon shot through the clouds, which gave a nice light to the streets. It was an exceptionally relaxed night to enjoy a stroll down the streets, or to kill the one person you yearned to see dealt with.

I stood just a few feet from the front door of the church as Gregory came around the side. "The coast is clear on the parameter," he said as he joined me.

We had decided to come to the church as we figured after killing the priest, Vlad had probably come to hide here where most people would never think never to look.

"Make sure he survives. I need answers before I kill him." I said as I began walking to the door.

"You ready?" Gregory asked me as he unholstered his pistol.

I didn't respond to him. All I did was unholster my pistol and open the door. That was response enough. I was focused and in my own world so I didn't even think to respond to him.

I opened the door slowly, which sent a low shriek into the nave of the church. We stepped inside with our pistols held firmly ahead of us, but it was dark and very hard to make out anything. The moonlight beamed in through the windows making some spots illuminated but not much. We stuck to those areas to avoid tripping over our feet as we made it to Father Edward's quarters.

We both stopped at the door as we stood back against the wall, one on each side of the door. I looked at Greg and nodded waiting for him to approve. He looked back at me and nodded in agreement as I burst through the door and pointed my gun around the room hoping to find Vlad. The room was empty and all I found was the murder scene. The room was a mess, the centre table was turned upside down, and everything was shifted around like there was a struggle. Still I found no Vlad.

"Damn!" I shouted as I kicked a book that lay at my feet.

Gregory knew why I shouted and didn't say a word as he looked around for any sign of Vlad being here.

"He's not here," I said as I stormed out of the room making my way back into the open area of the church. I perched myself on the altar and looked out into the benches where people would sit for endless hours just listening to the priest talk about the stories of the bible. Like people actually gave a shit about the priest or his Bible. They were sinners and fuck ups and probably only ran to God when they needed something for their own benefit. The little Christianity I had in me knew that's not the way this game worked. You didn't just beg when you needed something and received it. You had to earn it. For example, Vlad had earned a horrible death. You earn what you give out to the world-very different scenario but same concept none the less.

"There's not a speck of evidence showing he is here," Gregory said disconnecting me from my thoughts.

"I have no idea where he will go now," I stated in frustration. I looked up in disappointment and noticed a stairwell leading up to the church tower. I pointed up to the ladder which was elevated over a balcony in the back.

Gregory looked up to see where I was pointing and sighed. He holstered his pistol and began to make his way to the front door in search of a ladder. I too holstered my pistol and led him straight to the ladder which was nestled tightly behind an enormous statue of St. Michael the Archangel. The ladder rested on the statue's back and led straight up to the balcony. We climbed the balcony as quietly as we could and then unholstered our pistols just at the foot of the next ladder. The door latch was closed so the element of surprise would not work if he was up there.

"You ready?" I asked resting my hand on the fourth step of the ladder.

"As I will ever be."

I began slowly climbing up the ladder attempting to not make a sound. When I reached the top, I looked down at Gregory who was just beneath me ready to follow me up. The ladder looked so old I was surprised it could hold the weight of both of us without cracking. I looked up and used the nose of my pistol to lift the latch slowly. I peeked through the slit and saw a light on but no one was there. I lifted it slightly more to get a better look but again the coast seemed clear.

I could tell now that nobody was here so I opened the latch right over and stepped up as I collected myself. I holstered my gun and helped Greg up. He too holstered his gun as we looked out the wooden walkway of the tower where if the clock's arms stopped working, the repairmen could fix them. A gun cocked from across the room.

We swung ourselves around to see Vlad stepping into the light with his gun cocked as he appeared from behind one of the great wooden beams holding up the roof.

"You're always so close. But never close enough," Vlad said with a stupid grin dressed across his face.

"I'm not going to let you get away this time," I roared as I stepped forward.

Vlad raised his other hand addressing me to stop. "Both of you take your guns and toss them out the walkway to the street below," Vlad ordered.

I wanted him to feel in control so I did just as he said. I didn't need a gun, or a knife, or any weapon. I just needed my hands to finish him. I stepped back over to the walkway still facing Vlad and unholstered my gun. I reached behind me not even looking down and let it fall down to the street level. Greg too unholstered his pistol and dropped it down.

Vlad pulled up a chair and took a seat. "When I first killed your wife you were nothing but a regular unemployed man of America. Look at you now. You have nine kills under your belt if you include what the papers say about you killing Tom Finagin and your wife," he said as he giggled mockingly. "We all know it's seven... Oh wait and todays officer is eight, you even have a name. The Phantom Spree Killer. Very impressive."

I could hear the sarcasm in his voice and I just wanted to shut him up real bad.

"We all know your wife was killed by yours truly," he said as he grinned again like a fool addressing his pride in the fact. "Tom was killed by one of the Thieves so that couldn't be you either."

"The Thieves? What do the Forty Thieves have to do with the murder of my wife?" I asked in desperation.

"There's a lot you don't know, and you will never know," Vlad assured me.

I knew that if I wasn't careful I would be killed. But I had to beat the answers out of this man. I needed the truth. Even if I had to lie. "You can kill me, go ahead. Just tell me first who masterminded all this? What do the Thieves have to do with Evelyn's death?"

"You don't have the right to ask anything," Vlad said angrily.

I looked down and noticed the handle of my knife resting on my belt, slightly unconcealed from my jacket. I remembered throwing the knife at Annie. I wondered if I could throw the blade like that again and hit Vlad. It was too risky, but I had no other choice.

"Who are you, his killer buddy, his boyfriend? Vlad asked Gregory but more as a way of getting us upset to make a mistake. He was just waiting to have an excuse to kill us. I was going to give him one.

As Vlad was looking at Greg, I quickly reached in and grabbed the knife. While I threw it with all my might at Vlad. The first time I threw the blade at Annie was definitely a lucky hit. The blade this time went flying off to the side of the room like a dizzy bird hitting a wall. I leaped off to the side as Vlad shot at me. I hid behind one of the beams and then could hear Gregory and Vlad fighting. Another gunshot went off when I turned the corner rushing Vlad. Gregory dropped back to the ground, I rushed Vlad and knew Greg had been hit. I tackled Vlad back against one of the beams and we both awkwardly fell to the ground.

Vlad had dropped the pistol just a few feet away as he was leaning over me trying to reach it. My instincts were in full affect as I just needed to keep that man way from the gun. I bit Vlad's ear and tore half of it clean off spitting it onto the floor. Vlad screamed in pain as he reached and elbowed me in the nose. I could feel the blood pouring out all over my face as my breathing was distorted.

Vlad got up off the floor and began to relentlessly kick me in the ribs. After receiving a dozen blows to the mid-section, I tried to sweep him off his feet to stop the pain and was successful. He fell to the ground hard and I reached for the gun grabbing it.

I got up to my feet but was met by Vlad who held my wrist to the air while holding me tight. We both struggled and tried to overpower each other until Greg kicked at Vlad making us both stumble to the ground and I let go of the pistol. All three of us watched as the pistol slid across the ground and fell right off the walkway, dropping to the street below. There were no more guns as this would become nothing but a brawl. Gregory reached into his jacket and took out his knife.

Vlad shoved me off, sprinting over to Greg and kicking him in the face. Greg dropped the knife and grimaced in pain. I too rolled around on the ground as I was in a fair amount of pain myself. I could see Vlad grabbing the knife and then going over to the corner of the room and picking up the one I had failed to hit him with.

I looked over at Greg and noticed he was shot in the shoulder. It was one hell of a pain being shot in the arm as I knew that first hand, but at least it wasn't life threatening.

Vlad aggressively threw the knives out the walkway and turned to us. "No weapons, is that better?" he asked rhetorically. He walked over to me as I got up and was going to grab me but I uppercut him square in the jaw and he stumbled back. I got back on my feet and helped Greg back to his. I walked Greg over to a chair and helped him sit down as I turned over to Vlad.

Vlad was wiggling his jaw back and forth to help rearrange it back to normal. He grinned at me and pulled out a switchblade. He was a snake and the type of man to never play fair in a fight. I didn't fear him, his knife, or anything right now. I just wanted to see him dead, but first answer what I had wanted to know all along... Who had orchestrated Evelyn's death?

Vlad approached me while swinging the blade dangerously close as I attempted to veer from one side and then the next. He managed to cut my arm and the pain was excruciating. I could feel every moment of the blade making contact as my skin spread wide open. He cut right through the leather like it was butter. I stepped back and took my jacket off, I didn't care for the jacket, I just felt like it was heavy and in the way while I maneuvered around. I wanted to be light on my feet.

Vlad charged me again with the blade and this time didn't swing it. He thrusted it hard attempting to gut me but I shifted while hooking his extended arm with mine. I held him close in and punched him with my free hand in the ribs. After a few blows in rapid succession, I heard the blade drop to the ground. I then got the wind knocked out of me when Vlad tilted his head back and with all his might head butted me right in the forehead. My knees buckled but he held me up in the air as he swung and clocked me right in the cheekbone. I dropped hard to the ground and tried to sprawl back to my feet but Vlad came on top of me. I managed to slip my feet under his gut and shove him off me. I sprang up again but could feel the exhaustion hitting me hard. My body felt like lead, and I was having a hard time breathing since my face was badly beaten up.

Vlad charged me and tackled me with all his might. We fell into the latch door as it cracked, sending us down the ladder dropping to the balcony below. Vlad belted out a scream as he hit the statue.

I was the first to get to my feet, as I could see he had injured his leg and couldn't get up. I lay on top of Vlad and began choking him with both hands.

"Who were you working for?" I screamed slightly releasing my grip so he could use his vocal chords.

"I was working for your mother," he responded as he laughed.

I punched him across the face as the momentum slid my fist across the ground and I lay on him for a moment until hovering over him again. I could hear Gregory coming down the ladder now.

"You alright?" I asked as I looked over my shoulder and noticed he was bringing me Vlad's pocket knife.

"I've been shot worse believe me," Gregory said as he handed me the blade.

I pressed the edge of the blade against Vlad's throat. Vlad stiffened up in fear.

"I'm not going to ask you again. Who were you working for?"

"Ok...Ok... I was working for the Forty Thieves."

"More detail!" I shouted as I stabbed him in the thigh with the blade.

"Oh God, have mercy!" Vlad shouted as he grimaced, attempting to grab the wound.

If he was a good man, I would have felt sorry for the fool, but I didn't feel sorry, because he wasn't a good man and even though I had killed eight people and soon to be nine, he was a worse monster then I could ever become.

"You need to talk to their leader. He is the one that bought my services. He's the loan shark," Vlad said struggling to speak while in pain.

"A name, Give me a name!" I shouted as I pressed the blade against his neck.

Vlad looked me right in the eyes and took a big gulp that pressed his Adams apple against the blade drawing some blood. "Joseph Baker."

I let the blade drop as I got up to my feet and literally walked away stunned. The pussy of a man that I had just been with a few short hours ago was the one that had his own sister killed. I couldn't comprehend what was happening. I leaned over the balconies railing with my head dropped into my arms.

"What do you want to do with him?" Gregory asked me as he kept an eye on Vlad with the blade in hand.

I stood straight up looking at Vlad and walking by Greg as I grabbed the knife from his hand.

"Get up," I ordered.

Vlad slowly got up. "Don't do this man, I can get you to Joseph."

"You see my partner there," I said while pointing at Gregory with the blade of my knife. I turned Vlad around as he had his back to the balcony. "That is an ex Bowery Boy with a standing favor from them. I will get Joseph and all of his gang and, believe me, I will gut them all," I said as I kicked Vlad right over the balcony. He fell down into the open area. I looked down and could see one of his legs broken as he shouted in pain.

I slid down the ladder to the ground floor and approached him. I lifted him up and sat him at one of the benches facing the front altar in the back of the church.

"This is for capturing Grace," I said as I stabbed him in the gut.

He gasped for air but didn't make a sound.

"This is for Father Edwards, the priest of this church," I said as I stabbed him again in the gut.

He sat there barely making a sound as blood began to drool from his mouth unto his lap.

I grabbed him by the back of the neck and lifted his face to see me. I looked at him right in the eyes, "This... this is for my wife, Evelyn, who you stole from me!" I roared as I drove the blade right through the bottom of his jaw right up into his brain.

His eyes in a split second began to fade and I had finally killed Vlad. The man I had spent almost half a year with a vendetta to pay, was finally gone leaving me with the true mastermind of all this. My wife's own brother had her killed.

I sat beside the dead Vlad as I shoved him over and he lay his upper body onto the bench. I looked at the altar and just sat there with my thoughts.

Greg sat right next to me as he pulled in air to his lungs and held his breathe in an attempt to lessen the pain while holding his wound.

"To get your brother-in-law, we're definitely going to need to get through the Forty Thieves first."

"To kill an army, we first need an army," I replied as we both looked at the altar.

We got ourselves together and exited the church while looking for our weapons. They were laid out on the ground and we grabbed them. I had my jacket on again as it helped conceal my holstered pistol and knife. The jacket felt like a hundred pounds on my body right now but I preferred to wear it. I grabbed Vlad's gun and dropped it down into a sewer. We didn't want to hang around for too long because the cops would arrive any minute. Detective Murphy would be on our trail and we were honestly too exhausted to have to flee from him again. We stood under a tree at the park as rain began to spit from the sky and then progressively pick up.

"How are you going to get the Bowery Boys to go to war for us?" I asked almost yelling since the rain was trying to overpower my voice.

"I haven't figured that part out yet but just stay close to me and let me do all the talking."

"I won't argue with that" I said, I then continued, " I don't know these guys personally only from what the streets say about them."

"What the streets say is definitely true, believe me," Gregory agreed.

The rain began to stop and was back to just spitting so we began to walk.

"Your wound, will you be alright?" I asked while looking down at the poor job of bandaging it I had done.

"The Bowery Boys will fix it up once we get there, and besides the bullet went right through," Gregory assured me as we walked through the park using the cover from the moonlight by the trees as a way of walking freely.

CHAPTER 21: 6PM

I waited outside perched and leaning up against the wall of the Bowery with one guard on each side of me while Gregory was inside explaining our situation. The guards had stripped my gun and knife from my belt so I was unarmed. I was exhausted and really just wanted a place to sit as my legs were beginning to tremble. The night was on the warmer side but there was still a nice chill breeze passing by every so often. I looked out across the road and could see the Thieves building where they hung out. Joseph was in there, and every cell in my body wanted to run out across the Five Points open area and go in there and just blow his brains out. Obviously, it was much more difficult than that since he would have an army standing in front of him.

I needed my own army and that's why I had to wait out here patiently. Being patient and relying on someone else wasn't me. I always kept control of every situation, but I felt I could trust Gregory. He no longer had to aid me in this but yet here he was risking his neck for me. Getting shot would make most men run back under their mother's skirts— but not Greg.

The door to the Bowery opened and me and the guards and I looked over to see another Bowery Boy calling me in. I leaned off the wall and brushed passed a guard who didn't move as I walked by. When I walked in, I was led by the man while the two guards followed closely behind us.

I was led to a set of white doors. The man then said stuttering, "M-M-Mr.King w-w-will see you no-no-now," as he opened one of the doors.

I walked in and was greeted by none other than Gregory who was topless and had properly been bandaged up. He came to me to introduce me to, I was assuming, Roy King. I think that's what Gregory had said his name was. He was just behind his desk with his hands folded out in front of him. Four men were also next to him.

"This is Lawrence I was telling you about," Gregory said introducing me.

I approached the desk and stuck my hand out. Roy grabbed me by the wrist and pulled my head down to the desk hard. He held a blade down at my throat and reached in close. "Why the fuck should I not slit his throat and collect my one hundred from his bounty" Roy asked Gregory.

Gregory shot forward but not too close. "Easy, come on. You owe me a favor."

"Your favor was paid off when we patched up your arm," Roy said still holding me firmly.

"I have a proposition," I muttered as much as I could speak while having my face planted on the desk.

Roy held me but released his grip slightly— I'm sure just to hear what I had to say. "I'm listening," he said.

I scrambled to get free and he let me go since clearly, if he wanted me dead, the gang would have attacked me and finished me off.

"What's the bounty on my head alive?" I asked.

Everyone looked at each other confused.

Roy waved to one of his boys and they went into a cabinet and pulled out today's newspaper, handing it to him.

He read the page and then muttered in excitement, "three hundred dollars." All the boys in the room began cheering.

"You help me and I will turn myself over to you. You can have the money. I don't care. I just need to get my hands on Joseph," I explained.

"That's a great thought but.. I could just take you now," Roy said as he looked back at his boys and they all began to laugh.

"Roy, please don't do this. I have been part of the cause for a long time," Gregory explained.

"Gregory, my man, stay out of this before you get involved in this affair," Roy assured him and Gregory just stayed quiet.

Greg had warned me this could get bad and that is exactly what was happening. I couldn't try to run since, even if I fought off a few of the Boys, my bruised and battered body would collapse before I did any real damage. Then an idea sprang to me.

"I can get you to Owen Murphy if you do this for me," I said, knowing Roy wanted Owen for leaving the gang, many years ago. Thanks to Gregory for giving me that piece of information back at his house. But I was totally wondering why the hell I put that on the table since The detective wouldn't just walk with me down a deep dark alley.

"How are you going to do that?" Roy said with excitement drawn all over his face. I could tell I had his attention now so I just went along with it.

"I can take you to his daughter and use her as leverage to bring him from the shadows."

"You are not going to do that!" Greg shouted while trying to grab me.

I shoved Gregory off while Roy called a few of his dogs to hold him back.

I looked back at him and gave him a reassuring look to play along. I could tell he understood as he began to intensify his anger and make it look more real.

"Alright, Lawrence, Phantom, Mr. Talbot, whatever your fucking name is these days. You got yourself a deal," Roy said as he approached me with his arm extended it to handshake on it.

I accepted his shake with a firm grip and he just smiled at me. This was something Roy really wanted so I had to use it to my advantage.

"A week from now we will battle it out at the Five Points. I will declare the challenge at the court tomorrow."

I wanted to kill Joseph right at this moment but if I had waited months to discover who had done this to my Evelyn, I could definitely wait a week. I was prepared to let everything go but under these circumstances here I was ready to kill again. I finally knew who had planned it all. I needed energy and rest anyways as I probably couldn't even kill a fly with my body in this state.

"Stutter, take Lawrence here to his room," Roy ordered the man that had led me here.

"If you don't mind I would prefer the roof," I said looking at both of them.

Stutter looked over at Roy for his approval since he probably didn't take a shit without his boss's permission.

"Alright," Roy said and in an instant Stutter was out the door leading me upstairs.

I walked out on the roof and looked up at the moon which was ever so clear now that the rain had passed. The heat had dried most of the rain but there was still some wet patches.

"I-I-If y-y-you need any-any-anything, don't hesitate to a-a-ask" Stutter said.

"Alright, thanks. By the way," I said as he turned his back and began to walk. "What's your real name?"

"David," he replied, putting emphasis into his voice to blurt his name out in one shot. He then turned around and went down the steps.

I smiled, watching him leave and then found a dry patch by the edge of the roof which gave me a good vantage point of the Forty Thieves' hideout.

The time I spent with The Bowery Boys was very valuable as I learned close combat kills and sharpshooting. Roy was taking a liking to me as we were beginning to hang out most of the day together. I would go out with them and I had begun to make a kinship with all the gang members.

People spoke about them but they actually weren't all that bad. If you got to know them, you could see they were actually normal people just trying to survive. You had to ignore the street beatings and the political messages they sent to officials but it wasn't bad.

Today was the morning before the battle. The fight was to be held right in the middle of the Five Points at 6pm sharp. I'm sure Joseph was excited but he couldn't compare to my excitement, especially when he saw me on the battlefield. He would know I was on to him.

The door to the roof opened and I looked back to see Greg, David 'Stutter', and Roy coming towards me.

Roy had clothing folded out on his arm as they approached. Gregory was dressed up in the red shirt and the black pants with the red stripe down one leg— just like the Bowery Boys.

Roy extended his arm revealing to me just the same outfit. I looked down at my clothes and noticed they were in rags now.

"I'll keep my shirt but I'll take the pants," I said grabbing them from Roy's arm.

"You're one of us today, Lawrence, so we want you to be dressed like it. The pants will do fine. If you want the shirt, it's here for you," he said as he placed it down.

"How's your arm?" I asked looking at Gregory.

"It's ready for today," he said smiling and slightly moving it.

"Also, no guns in today's fight. So keep your pistols in the Bowery before we head out," Roy stated.

I nodded in agreement but honestly didn't like the idea of the Colt staying behind.

"It's just a few hours," Roy said, placing his hand on my shoulder. "Then you can get your revenge," he said as he turned his back and walked away with David.

"I don't like the idea of not having my pistol on me," I said looking out to the street where many people were shopping. You could tell everyone was nervous as they were shopping quickly for the things they needed before the fight. When there was going to be a gang war, people never wanted to be outside when that was going to happen.

"It's the rules, and you got what you want. You got your army so just follow them," Gregory said as he patted me on the back and then went downstairs.

Sometime later, I exited the Bowery now representing the gang with my striped pants and I walked out onto the road. I unholstered my pistol and looked back at the Bowery. Nobody was watching me since the few guards hanging out were just focused on talking about the tail they had banged the night before, and seeing who had the best one. Such useless talk but hey, it gave me the opportunity I needed to stash my gun just in case I needed it.

I buried it right in front of the Thieves' hideout, right by a lamp post. Luckily, it had rained that morning and the soil was soft so it was done quickly before anyone had noticed. I then walked back to the Bowery and waited upstairs on the roof.

I sat upstairs with my thoughts the entire time. What did I want to say to Joseph before I killed him? What did I want him to know? It was 5pm and the streets were deserted. I swear, when these brawls were going to happen, even the animals sensed the tension since they never came around.

Gregory came up to call me. "Lawrence, it's time," he said as he approached me. "Just so you know, Grace is back at my home waiting for you. I got one of my sources to get in touch with her."

"Thank you," I answered firmly while we walked downstairs. At this point, my heart was beating very rapidly. I was nervous and I was hungry for vengeance. Grace was the least of my worries now that I knew Evelyn had been murdered by her own blood. I would need to do this to be able to move on. This closure was not what I had expected it to be. I thought it was just another Joe that had planned it and I would kill him like I did all the others and be done with it. This was much deeper. Family killing family, that was not right.

"Alright, everyone," Roy said addressing the entire gang that was standing in the open part of the Bowery. Roy was standing up on a stage overlooking us all.

"Lawrence, come up here," Roy called to me.

All eyes stared at me. I did just as I was told. I climbed up on the stage.

"Lawrence has one target in mind and that is Joseph Baker, the Forty Thieves leader. No one in this room will kill him except this man. If you have the opportunity to you bring him to Lawrence, then do it. In exchange for this, he has offered to turn himself in to the police and we get the ransom," Roy explained as everyone cheered.

Roy raised his hand to the roof to silence the crowd. I could see Greg had not cheered and just watched on.

"We will not turn Lawrence in," Roy explained. I looked at him in shock—hell everyone in the Bowery was in shock.

Roy looked over at me and grinned while giving me a half hug. "He is one of us, and we don't turn our back on our own," he shouted as he raised his arm. The whole gang cheered loudly into the air. This time, Gregory got involved as he was shouting with the gang.

"Now let's get out there and either kill em' all, or die with honor!" Roy screamed as the gang shouted even louder. Everyone moved aside making way for Roy to walk. Everyone was ready with weapons in hand. Some people carried knives, clubs, axes, anything they could carry to kill the enemy.

Roy walked through the crowd and I followed. David, and Gregory joined us at the front.

We made our way through the Bowery. Once we were just a few short steps from the door, I removed my jacket and placed in on a wooden box near the broken window.

We walked outside and made our way to the center of the Points. We waited.

The door to their hideout opened up and the Forty Thieves, which was clearly a lie since there was more like a hundred fifty of those bastards, walked out. We were outnumbered at least two to one. I could see Joseph standing in the middle of the wall of men as he looked around and spotted me.

"What are you doing here?" he asked in confusion.

"Vlad," was all I said, I clenched my teeth and began to step forward. Roy extended his arm and held me back.

"You have patiently waited for months. Now just wait one minute and nobody will stop you," Roy said. He walked forward and met Joseph in the center of the street. The two talked to each other.

I was feeling a rage. I looked over at Greg who was just a few feet from me. "He's all yours," he simply said. I looked back at Joseph who was approaching his gang again.

"Alright, today one gang will be obliterated in front of the state of New York. Let the land of America decide our fate!" Roy screamed out and both gangs cheered.

I grabbed a pair of knives I had at my waist which were being held by my belt and raised them in the air. as I began to cheer with everyone.

As the two gangs stared out at each other in silence, I got the opportunity to live in the shoes of warriors of history. History you would hear from teachers about the great wars of the middle age where knights and warriors would travel the world slaying each other with huge swords. My swords were no more than five inches but it would have to do. I didn't want to carry a mace or an axe—those weapons slow a person down. I wanted to be in and out before my enemy could breathe.

Joseph inhaled and then released an outburst. "KILL THEM!" and both armies ran to each other with everything they had.

CHAPTER 22: MASS MURDER

As both gangs charged, roaring violently, I ran into a beast of an Irishman. He came at me with a mace of sorts. The killing point was a huge stone tied to a stick by some leather rope. He swung across trying to take my head clear off. I ducked down and drove my knife into his leg. The shank didn't seem to faze him. I pulled the blade out and stepped back. The bear of a man took the momentum of the swing and pulled the mace up to the sky and drove down over me. I leapt back throwing myself completely to the ground to avoid that murderous blow.

As I attempted to rise to my feet, still keeping my eyes on the monstrous man, another Irishman came at me with a knife. I lay back down and used his momentum against him. I grabbed his arm pulling him in and kicked his mid-section with my foot while rolling him through the air over my head. I reached over while sprawling and drove my blade into his heart. I looked over my shoulder to see the stone edged mace tearing through gravity once more. I leapt away to safety. I stabbed the same leg through the calf this time and again the man was unfazed. He used his free hand to grab me by the shirt and pick me up, still holding the mace in the other hand.

He attempted to head butt me but I kicked him in the inside of the knee, which made him slightly buckle. I used that time to stab him with both knives in the chest. He released his grip of me, which I was sure was due to some pain. No matter how big a man or small, pain was pain. Eventually, though some can tolerate more than others, everyone would bleed and die the same.

I held the really bloody knives now since my hands were covered in this ogre's blood. His legs seemed wobbly and I knew I almost had him. I didn't want to get too close since his grip was unfathomable and I would be much safer. I flipped one knife over and held in my the pointed end. I whipped the knife at the beast of a man and hit him in the neck. I could see him dropping his weapon and grabbing his throat. His eyes rolled far back into his head and he dropped to the ground. Another Irishman ran at me. I met him halfway and I ducked under. I rose up quickly, head butting the bottom of his chin. He was severely dazed and was no challenge for me as I drove my knife into his gut. He bled from the mouth and dropped dead almost instantly. I ran back to collect my other knife, which was done doing its job on the beast.

I was used to killing people but as I looked around I could see so much blood, and so much death. I felt overwhelmed at the slaughter I was witnessing with my own eyes. I stood there in a daze for a moment. I came out of it and looked around so I wouldn't get shanked from my blind side. I could see Roy and Greg going to work on the enemies.

Where was Joseph? I looked around and could not see him in the midst of the battle. I walked around trying to find him and then noticed a Bowery Boy laying on the ground trying to hold an Irishman off of him. He held the man's wrists. The man who was using all his weight to drive the blade into him. I wasted no time and whipped the blade. Which drove right into the back of the Irishman, who panted and slightly let go of his attacker. I reached over and grabbed my blade. I drove it several times into his back while still looking around the street for Joseph.

"I owe you one," the Bowery Boy said.

I tossed the blade over to my other hand now holding both and reached my free hand out to help him to his feet. He took my hand and continued on to the next enemy like nothing happened.

I could now see Joseph who was at the border of the battle like the coward he was. I began to make my way over to him when suddenly the roar of footsteps and chariots approached. Everyone stopped what they were doing and looked over at the site of the entire police department standing in formation. Both gangs combined were still outnumbered two to one. I could see Detective Murphy coming to the front of the formation with something in his hands. I reached in closer to look and noticed he was carrying a megaphone.

As the Detective walked out, he waved his free hand up in the air and the chariots began to turn around. The chariots were guided back now as there was one on each end of the formation. Two officers on each chariot lifted off the top of the back of each. What was inside was something out of a nightmare. The stories you would only hear about the battlefields of war. On each chariot manned by two officers was an 1861 Model Gatling Gun.

Detective Murphy wore an over-exaggerated smile on his face at the revealing of the murder machines. He then pressed the megaphone to his lips.

"I'm extremely tired of having to deal with gangs and thugs who waste too much valuable time in taking care of the city the way it should be taken care of. I turn a lot of my attention to the people who are victims of kidnapping, and rape, and murder—but when someone kidnaps my family that is a different story. I could order you all to disperse but that will not help this city."

Roy stepped forward. "So what detective, are you saying you're going to slaughter us all? You know very well that the police department shouldn't get involved in the affairs of the Five Points."

Detective Murphy gave a chuckle. "You're right. But when my daughter was kidnapped by you worthless pieces of shit and, to top it off, you house a wanted killer and fugitive of our beautiful country, where does that leave the police department?"

Roy stood strong trying to keep the officers off of our fight while Joseph, the supreme leader of the Irish, was hanging out in the corner ready to run. "I apologize on the behalf of the Bowery Boys but we had nothing to do with the kidnapping of your daughter— that was the Irish," Roy proclaimed, pointing at a few Irishmen that stood near him.

Detective Murphy reached back and grabbed a rifle from the hands of a nearby officer. He dropped the megaphone down to the ground and lifted the rifle towards Roy. Roy raised his arms, shocked and not sure how the police department was allowing the murder of cold blood out on the streets.

Detective Murphy shouted then while looking back at his department. "On my go. 3...2...1...FIRE!" When he finished the sentence, bullets began to rain towards everyone on the field. I quickly lay to the ground. I could see Murphy shooting Roy. It was continued by a barrage of bullets that sent The Bowery leader pummeling to the ground. Roy wasn't the only one to get shot. Everyone was getting peppered with bullets. It was a mass murder.

The officers shot their rifles and then moved to the back of the formation. A new row of officers then came to fire theirs. The worst part was the Gatling guns had not started firing yet. If they fired, everyone would be obliterated.

I looked around for the lamp post in front of the Thieves' hideout and spotted it. I needed my gun, but I also needed the courage to get up and dodge the countless bullets soaring through the air. Many of the survivors were now hiding behind cover. I thought of Evelyn and Grace, held my breath hard and leapt up to my feet. I sprang forward with all my might. I could hear a few bullets flying by me but I persisted on to the lamp post. I was glad I had very calmly placed the dirt on top of the gun. If it had been packed dirt there was no way in hell I could have dug it out in time.

"Shoot the fugitive," the detective belted. I could now hear the spinning of metal.

I looked over to see the Gatling guns spinning and quickly reached into the dirt pulling up the pistol. I ran into the Thieves' hideout while an absolute storm of bullets shot into the wall I had just passed through.

I jumped over the stairs stomach first onto the dusty ground beneath me. The sound of bricks, wood, and glass shattering echoed very loudly through the building. I covered my ears and head from the flying debris. The bullets began to lessen until they were shooting the gangs outside.

I rolled over and looked up at the steps where there used to be a wall. There was now an opening view to the sky.

I could hear movement in the building and pulled all of my attention to my next target, the man who had done all this to me, to Evelyn.

I made my way in slowly through piles of boxes while I held my pistol tightly ahead of me. The boxes were like cardboard mountains. It was difficult to see since they were lined up like corridors. I focused with all my might to hear the sounds of footsteps. When there was a noise, I would press on closer to where it came from. I heard a shuffling just a few feet ahead of me to the right. I tightened the grip of the pistol and took a deep gulp. I swung myself around the cardboard corner with pistol leading the charge. I was startled since I expected Joseph, but in return all I got was a cat.

"Jesus Christ!" I shouted then instantly covering my mouth with both hands. I wish I hadn't screamed, but I had. The element of surprise was gone. It was alright. I didn't need it anyway.

I began to sneak my way through again until I came to the back area of the warehouse. I could see Joseph making his way up the wooden steps. They sounded like they would crack under the weight of a person. I reached for my jacket pocket to load up my gun but I realized I had left my jacket across the street at the Bowery. I opened the spindle of the gun and noticed I had four bullets left. That would be more than enough. I closed the gun back and cocked it.

I ran towards the steps and looked upstairs, trying to be cautious not to get shot in the back when I ran up. I didn't know if he had a weapon by now or which type of weapon. A gun would be obvious now that he was back in the Bowery but I would have to be cautious.

I ran up while looking around and noticed his shadow from a dim light next to him. The fool was trying to hide and was definitely failing at that. I crept my way over to the box that stood before me and the man that had changed my entire life.

"I know you're hiding there so come out," I ordered, pointing the pistol at him.

Joseph walked out from behind the box with his hands in the air while he kept his eyes on the ground. He knew he was caught and that this wouldn't turn out well for him. I pointed my gun signaling for him to take a seat on that same box he hid behind and he did just that.

I approached my beloved 'brother-in-law.' I was ready to end his life when the sound of running footsteps echoed through the huge building. I ran and looked over the railing to see Detective Murphy looking up at me. He shot at me which rang off of the metal railing. I shot back behind cover while looking over at Joseph, who was running down the hall into a room, the only room upstairs. I sprinted towards the door and attempted to open it but Joseph had locked it behind him. I tugged the door knob relentlessly but I was stopped.

"Drop the gun, and put your hands where I can see them," Detective Murphy ordered. His hands shook with excitement or paranoia. I honestly couldn't tell. I didn't know what to think of this situation since the detective wasn't a bad person. He was just one of those officers that stuck to the books. Now on the other hand, I think the line that kept him sane was cracked since Grace had been abducted. Would he kill me? Hell yes, he would. He just mowed down over a hundred people. Why wouldn't he kill the one person that had slipped from his fingers time and time again?

CHAPTER 23: CORNFIELD

I watched helplessly as the detective held my life in his hands. I was used to being in complete control. Hell, I'm a control freak, so feeling powerless like I did was out of my comfort zone.

"This is the end of the road for you, Phantom," the detective said while he edged up forward, only a few steps between us.

"Don't do this, Owen. You're a good man. There's no coming back from murder," I explained, hoping to save my own life.

"Don't..." he started to speak then closed his eyes tight, twitching his head. The Detective was definitely not right in the head at the moment. He then tried again. "Don't call me Owen. We're not on a first name basis, you hear me?"

"Alright, Detective. Understood. Let's just take it easy now," I answered as I dropped my gun to the ground slowly. I then continued to raise my hands.

I felt an almost uncontrollable joy grow inside me that nourished my very soul. I could see Greg slowly making his way behind Owen. Poor Owen never had any idea that his friend was about to shut the lights on him. Greg gave a stiff blow with his bat to the back of Owen's head. You could see he put just enough to knock his friend out but not enough to kill him. The detective crashed to the ground like a ton of bricks.

I crouched down and grabbed my pistol from the ground.

"Thanks," I muttered

"You go on ahead and do what you have to. I'll tie up our friend here," Greg said. He was already grabbing Owen and propping him up against a beam.

I holstered my weapon and walked over to Greg, sticking my hand out, the way we first met. He shook my hand but had a look of confusion.

"What's this for?" he asked while he shook my hand hard.

"I just want to thank you, Greg, for everything you have done up to this point for me, and for Grace."

"You're a good person, Lawrence. You just had bad things happen to you. You handled it the best way you could. You may have lost yourself for a while but I know you found your way back. Now go in that room and serve justice—to your soul."

I smiled and then broke out in tears. I hadn't cried in such a long time, since before the coma. My feelings rushed me. Justice would finally be served so that Evelyn could rest if she was watching.

I approached the door of the room and grabbed the knob. I was surprisingly calm but I still hesitated to try and open the door again. I waited a brief moment and then kicked at the door. The door wouldn't budge so I pointed the barrel of the gun at the knob and looked away, shooting it clean off.

I could hear Joseph give a yelp as I released the bullet. I kicked the door in hard and pounced in as I looked for the snake. I walked over to him with my gun in hand and he dropped to his knees begging for mercy. "Please I beg you, don't kill me."

"Get the fuck up," I ordered. I looked away in disgust. This isn't how I had imagined I would serve the final justice, to a whimpering dog begging for his life.

I heard a movement and looked down to see Joseph hit me with something in the face. Whatever it was hurt like hell. I stumbled back a few feet and then shook my head to adjust my blurry vision. I now noticed he held a little pipe with both hands.

I wiped the blood from my mouth and grinned. I holstered my gun again. I pulled out the two knives I had just used to slay three Irishmen. You could tell as they were still bloodstained.

"Before I kill you, tell me why you did this to me and your sister."

"You want answers that you will never get. You will never get that satisfaction I can guarantee you that," Joseph replied mockingly while he swung the pipe around.

I could tell he was trying to show off his moves with the pipe but I didn't give a shit. I had killed many people and I was sure this little bitch of a man was nothing extraordinary. I rushed forward and thrusted but Joseph shot back and hit my hand with the pipe. The pain was like a piercing through the flesh that made my hand jerk open unintentionally. I dropped the knife and clasped my hand slightly with my other, still holding the other blade.

Alright, so he was pretty good. I would give him that but nonetheless, he wouldn't make it out alive.

I ran in quick and low. Just by Joseph's movements, I could tell he didn't expect that as I came from under his swing and hit him right in the jaw with the top of my head. I wanted to kill him with every cell in my body, but not until I had the answers I wanted. I just hoped I didn't break his jaw which would make speaking an impossible task.

He stumbled to the ground and the pipe rolled a safe distance away.

"Oh shit," he muttered. Which was a great relief to hear. His jaw was in fact not broken.

I was tired of playing games and withdrew my pistol. I pointed in close to his head while he was crawled for his weapon. "Game over, Joseph. Speak or die."

"You won't kill me," he said laughing.

I pointed my gun at his leg and shot him. The laughing would stop, I'm certain, and it did.

"Alright, alright. God you fucking shot me. God," he whimpered like the bitch he was.

"Next time, will be in the balls. I assure you."

"Alright, alright, I get it. I'm not dying for this shit anymore man," he explained holding his hands between his face and my gun.

"What shit?"

"This shit. The murder, the money it's all planned," he stated.

"I know you planned it but that's what I want to know. Why did you do it?"

Joseph grabbed his leg and pressed the wound in keeping the blood inside his leg as much as possible. He grimaced but then found the strength to continue speaking, "I didn't fucking plan it, I swear."

"What are you talking about? Vlad said it was you."

"If shit got hairy, he was to say I planned all this but I didn't, Lawrence, I swear. Yes I knew you couldn't have been killed by the priest so I spread a rumor out on the street about me owing Vlad money. That was the only thing I truly planned. We wanted you dead and what would be easier then bringing you to us."

My palms were sweaty, knees were weak, and my arms were heavy I couldn't comprehend who was behind all this then. Everything was planned accordingly. I needed the answers right now. I couldn't wait any longer so I pressed the barrel of the pistol right up against his other leg to inject the amount of fear I needed for a quick answer. "Who is it? Who ruined my life?"

"I think you should go out to the person's home and see for yourself. I'm done with this. I'm not dying," he proclaimed in an unfathomable amount of pain.

I reached down and grabbed Joseph by the collar, lifting him up onto his one good foot.

"I won't kill you if you take me to this place," I said.

Joseph's eyes watered with tears of joy. "Alright, I have a chariot in the back. Let's go there," he explained.

I walked out of the room carrying Joseph by one arm while he limped out. I looked over at Greg who was sitting on a crate. The detective looked over at me and damn, he looked like hell.

"I heard everything, Lawrence. Let me handle this situation. I can't let you be a free man for killing innocents but I can make you avoid the death penalty." The detective said as he looked up at me tied to a wooden beam. I couldn't tell if he was lying but I didn't care nonetheless.

"I appreciate that Detective but I must solve this ordeal on my own. I will hand myself in to your custody once this is all over."

"Lawrence, no more bloodshed," the detective said firmly.

"Blood will spill once more," As I muttered those words in response, I walked to the back with Joseph and we made it down the long wooden stairs.

I helped Joseph into the caravan, which by help I meant practically threw him inside. I jumped in the front and lightly whipped the horses to begin moving. "Where are we headed?" I asked while looking back at a small window in the caravan.

"New Jersey. A New Jersey Farm," Joseph said.

"A farmer planned all this?" I asked confused

Joseph let out a sigh. "You have no idea."

We spent a good two hours making our way out of New York and into New Jersey territory. The road was dirt and dust now and there was nothing but farmland as far as the eye could see. The sun was well on its way as the night was beginning to creep in. The sky was a beautiful shade of pink.

"Over there, on your left," Joseph said as I stopped the carriage with a sudden halt.

I tugged on the horses hard and pushed the carriage slowly off the road to the left. I quickly climbed the carriage roof and looked out into the home where I could see someone walking across his or her front porch. It was a fair distance away and so I couldn't make out just who it was exactly.

I climbed down and opened the door.

"Hey, now. I'm not going out there. That wasn't part of the deal," Joseph said as he slid back into the carriage for me not to reach him. I climbed up and reached in with half my body. I grabbed him and tossed him onto the dirt floor outside the carriage.

"The deal was I don't kill you if you bring me to the culprit. Don't make me change my mind" I explained clapping my hands together to release the dust attached to my palms.

"I'm a dead man anyways, once I'm seen," Joseph muttered. He spit on ground while getting back up to his feet. He then gagged and spit again and I realized he wasn't spitting because he was disgusted. He was spitting because he had literally eaten dirt when I threw him outside the carriage cabin.

I giggled and Joseph looked back at me confused. I rubbed my now growing beard and looked down the road towards the direction of the house. I reached back and closed the carriage door while Joseph stayed in the same spot. He knew he couldn't run or I would shoot him dead so he stayed, like a good little doggie. I grabbed the straps of the carriage and tied the horses to a nearby tree. I grabbed Joseph and threw his arm over my shoulder once more. "Let's get going before it's dark," I said and began taking him.

"You're in a real hurry to die," he said.

We reached the fork in the road which was a dirt path leading to the farmhouse. I stood still for a moment scoping out the scene while still holding Joseph up. His wounded leg was bleeding right down to the dirt.

I looked down to see the blood. "Don't die just yet. You're almost a free man," I stated as I looked up at the house again. The house was fairly big, and very white. The field I had to walk across was no more than one hundred feet. That wasn't much of a hike at all, but when I as carrying a half dead man on my shoulders that could become quite troublesome.

"It's your lucky day," I said while I helped Joseph down to a sitting position.

"It's your most unlucky day, friend," he responded. He chuckled and then quickly replaced it with a pant of exhaustion or pain as he grabbed his wounded leg.

I turned my focus to the house and began walking through the cornfield at a steady pace while I tried to control my breathing to calm my nerves.

I was nervous. Every step I took reaching the house become harder but I pushed on. This nightmare I had been ensnared in was finally coming to an end. Four months of brutal hell and whoever was in this nice, white home was the mastermind behind it all. I thought it was Vlad which I was wrong. Then I thought it was Joseph which also was a mistake. I knew deep down inside in my gut that this was it. This was the end of it all. I would finish this for good and then turn myself into the police. I didn't care what happened to me after. It was pretty clear at this point, I would definitely hang for what I had done to Ben, Annie, and all those other people but I didn't give a shit about that. I just wanted justice for Evelyn.

I reached the front of the house and slowly crouched and made my way to the home. I could hear more then one person speaking. It sounded like a woman and a man but that didn't make any sense. I practically crawled to the front door and took a quick glimpse inside. I couldn't tell exactly who was there but I could definitely hear a female and male voice. I turned around the edge of the door and sat against the wall looking out into the infinite cornfields.

Who in the hell was in the house? I couldn't waste any more time. I was about to get up and the front door swung open. Out stepped Conor. I didn't even move a muscle. I just stood there shocked. I thought Joseph said Conor had died?

"Sweetie, there's enough corn in here," said a familiar female voice as she walked out of the door. Her dark hair swaying against the glass. The voice was too familiar. I looked up and my heart stopped. Evelyn was the female walking through the door. Evelyn, my dead wife.

CHAPTER 24: PLAYED A FOOL

I looked at Evelyn from head to toe. Her body was very similar to the way I remembered, though she had put on a few pounds. The few pounds were definitely because of the baby. I could see that clearly as her stomach was showing well into the final months.

Joseph had said that the people who ruined my life were the people in the farmhouse but how could Evelyn do all this? It didn't make any sense, and why did she call Conor sweetie?

I planted my hand against the white wall and forced myself to my feet. I unholstered my pistol and walked to the edge of the porch while I watched Conor and Evelyn kiss.

"Who is going to explain what the fuck is happening here?" I said as I raised my gun at Conor.

Evelyn and Conor were passionately kissing with their eyes closed but that quickly stopped as both of their eyes opened wide and they slowly turned their faces to see me.

I could see Evelyn's face. She was as white as a ghost.

"You were supposed to be dead," she muttered to me.

"I was supposed to be dead? Speak for yourself, though you look very alive and in the hands of this dip shit."

"This wasn't supposed to play out like this Eve," Conor said as he looked at her with a look of resentment.

"Eve? Don't make me vomit. Both of you get your asses in the house now! I want answers."

Evelyn walked in first and Conor followed. I kept very close to them both as I walked in, shutting the door behind me.

Conor was going to sit but I preferred he stay standing. As he pulled up a chair and went to sit I reached in and kicked the chair from under him, sending him crashing butt first to the ground. I could see it in his eyes that he wanted to attack me but the pistol reminded him who was in charge.

I looked over at Evelyn still trying to grasp that this wasn't just a messed up dream. Then the door of the house opened and Joseph stepped in.

"How could you not kill him?" Evelyn said as she looked furiously at her brother.

"Kill me? I'm confused didn't you love me?" I interrupted.

Evelyn laughed aloud, mocking me to my face. "Love you? My God, no. I was so tired of you. I just needed a way out. You know in today's society, if a man leaves a woman that's ok but God forbid a woman left a man. She is a slut for all eternity."

"How long did you plan to ruin my life?" I asked.

"For quite some time you see. I fell in love with Conor a few months before and it was his idea to separate from you but I had to come up with a sure way to make it happen."

"The last time we had dinner at your parents... Oh my God," I said. I covered my mouth with my hand looking down to the ground.

"What is it?" Joseph asked.

"That time you told him to get his hands off of my wife, they were already... Wait, is that even my child? We couldn't have kids and then..." I asked confused.

"Evelyn, just tell the fool already," Conor said while he got back up to his feet.

Evelyn shot a sigh and then said it coldly. "I'm pregnant with Conor's baby."

I screamed and ran at Conor, grabbing him by the hair. He whimpered but couldn't do much. I tossed him around like a doll, still holding his hair fully in my hands. I holstered the pistol and began punching his face repeatedly. Evelyn came to break us up but Joseph held her back. I looked around and saw some rope against the far wall. I reached in and grabbed it, still holding Conor by the hair.

I laid Conor on the dinner table and began to tie him down. Joseph helped me and soon Conor was helpless since he couldn't move.

Joseph collapsed to the ground. I looked up and noticed Evelyn had stabbed Joseph in the back. She reached down and stabbed him multiple times. I ran around the table and grabbed her, tossing her aside but it was too late—Joseph was already dead. I reached over in a pit of rage and backhanded Evelyn hard to the ground. I grabbed her and sat her on a chair. She whimpered but didn't try to fight back. I pulled out my knife and cut some of the left over rope that was holding down Conor. I tied her to the chair and knew she would not be stabbing me in the back while I did my business.

I grabbed Conor's leg while he watched me in horror. "Don't kill me," he begged as I slit the knife right up his leg almost to his groin. His pants split and I lifted the material up, slicing the rest in half until he was laying butt naked on the table.

I could just cut his balls off but I didn't think that was proper pain to give someone who had caused me so much pain in return. I went outside and looked around for something 'suitable'.

I saw what put a huge smile on my face— a hammer and a bucket of huge steel nails for fences. The nails looked similar to what they said was put through Jesus Christ's hands to hold him up on the cross. I grabbed the hammer and two of the nails and made my way back inside.

Conor began to tremble as he saw me walk in with my new toys.

"Holy shit! Holy shit! Evelyn say something," Conor begged.

I laughed while I lay the hammer and nails between his legs on the table.

"Don't do this to us. Please, Lawrence," Evelyn pleaded.

"Lawrence is dead. I am the Phantom," I replied in brutal honesty— my human self had disappeared from this world forever.

"You will tell me everything from the beginning or Conor will get nailed nuts," I said boldly.

"JESUS FUCKING CHRIST!" Conor shouted as he cried aloud.

"Ok, I'll start from the beginning," she said calmly.

I lay back against the table prepared to listen to the truth.

"Everything that happened to you was planned by me. I got a lot of money from a theft the Thieves had made from and since Joseph was the leader, he got the biggest cut. The Commissioner of State was paid off to fire you and give me half your severance pay."

"Who kept the other half?" I inquired.

"The commissioner would keep it. That way you would be forced to do whatever you had to get us money. For the next step, was where I planned with Joseph for you to talk to him, which you very easily fell for, and he would lead you to the loan shark, Vlad."

"My God, you're a monster," I interrupted.

"I knew you would not be able to keep a job since times were hard. This would make it impossible to pay Vlad back the money we lent you, which was actually your severance pay— isn't that ironic?" She asked giggling.

"Just continue," I said, trying to compose myself as much as I could to get the full story.

"I was sick which wasn't part of the plan. But it was actually me getting pregnant, which I had known for a while, that made it work out perfectly to burn through our last bit of money much quicker. The night of Tom's death, it was Conor who would set you up while Vlad, his goons and me would set up the apartment with Joseph in case we needed a plan B. Since you didn't get arrested, we had you dazed in the apartment. This was perfect. Joseph tossed the pig blood to Vlad, who played the stabbing perfectly and poured the blood on me at the same time. Joseph fled through the kitchen window and everyone else you saw them leave."

"The coroner said you were dead?." I stated.

"It's amazing how just about anyone will do your will if you pay them some money," she snickered.

I loved Evelyn with every part of my body and soul and I was sure she felt the same for me. Clearly, I had no clue who she truly was. I propped myself up and looked at Conor coldly.

"She told you the truth, man. Let us go now," Conor said hoping to win me over.

"I need you to feel pain," I answered simply.

"Evelyn, help!" Conor belted. I walked around the table and grabbed one nail and the hammer.

I pressed the nail up against one of Conor's testicles while he squirmed and cried out loud worse than a child who couldn't have that one chocolate bar. I raised my arm up looking at his face and felt the joy of what I was going to do to him.

I could hear him begging but at this point my ears were ringing and my heart was pounding. I thrusted the hammer with all my might against the head of the nail and a huge POP! sound sent Conor into a convulsion. He foamed from the mouth. A steady stream of blood began to flow across the table. I hit the head of the nail again and again until the nail had completely popped his testicle and was jabbed through the table. I smiled wide and looked at Evelyn, who was wearing a terrified look.

"Only one more to go," I said mockingly while I grabbed the other nail.

"Stop this!" Evelyn shouted but I ignored her. I found the lonely ball and WHAM! I hit the second nail with all my might. This time, the pop sound wasn't as loud. I pulled the nail out, holding the bloody piece of steel in my hand.

I walked around the table and stood over Conor. He looked at me with a broken soul of a face. His body shivered and he just whimpered while his voice had left him. I pressed the tip of the nail right into the spot between his nose and his eye and he just mumbled to me. I'm sure he was begging me not to but I didn't care to listen.

"Justice is served," I said. I hammered the nail right through Conor's skull. Once the nail had passed his face, I kept hammering his face in until he was practically headless.

I held the bloody hammer while I approached Evelyn, who was as white as snow. She just began to cry. I untied her from the chair but kept her bound by her hands and escorted her outside and across the field. She attempted to talk to me multiple times but she never got a response out of me. I sat her inside the carriage Joseph and I had come in and looked at her while I held the door.

"The only reason I'm sparing you is because of the baby, or I would do far worse to you than Conor," I said. I slammed the door and stepped up to the front of the carriage.

Evelyn screamed and shouted at the top of her lungs. I jumped down and opened the carriage door, slicing a piece of my sleeve and gagging her with it. I no longer needed to hear her voice and I no longer needed my shirt looking nice. I was turning myself and the real monster in to Detective Murphy. Real justice would be served.

CHAPTER 25: GAME OVER

The moon was now shining in the night sky with all its glory as I stopped the carriage at the Five Points intersection. I could see the police department moving the bodies around, after the brutal massacre. I stepped down from the carriage and approached an officer who was blocking the street.

"My lord sir, what has happened here? I asked acting oblivious.

"This is a police matter and you have nothing to worry about. Now get on home."

"I have actually come here to speak to Detective Murphy. Is he around?" I asked looking out to all the dead bodies.

"The detective currently has his hands full at the moment but I could leave a message if you like."

"That would be greatly appreciated. Just let him know the Phantom is waiting here for him," I said and the cop's face turned as pale as the moonlight.

The officer was reaching for his gun. "Don't do that. I can draw mine much quicker believe me. Just do your duty and tell him I need to speak to him," I ordered and the officer ran to get Detective Murphy.

I walked calmly back to the carriage and opened the door. Evelyn shot me a glare of complete hatred, while I returned a joyous mocking smile. I was smiling because I didn't want her to see my real feelings towards her. If she wasn't pregnant, I would gut the bitch and make her eat her intestines.

I could hear approaching steps as I looked back and could see the detective and a handful of officers approaching me. The detective held his hand firmly to the sky and the officers stopped behind him. Everyone had their pistols drawn and so I decided to unholster mine also.

"Drop the pistol."

"I am turning myself in," I said calmly, cutting the detective off as he spoke.

"You have got to be kidding me?"

"I am not," I said while I lowered my pistol slowly, holding it out with only my thumb and index finger. I crouched down and placed it on the ground and then kicked it over to the officers.

"Grab his gun," Detective Murphy ordered one of the officers and he did just that. "Check him for weapons," he said and another officer ran to my side to grab my knife from my belt.

"I assure you the two weapons you see are all I carry." I quickly grabbed the officer while he was checking me and hid behind him, controlling him by the throat. My arm was wrapped around his throat hard as I shifted myself over to the door of the carriage.

"Let my officer go. What do you want?" Detective Murphy inquired in desperation.

"I'm just making sure I survive long enough to show you my gift to you, and to the entire country," I said. I let the officer go pushing him forward and jumped into the carriage. Evelyn tried to squirm her way free but I grabbed her by the hair and dragged her out. I tossed her to the ground putting her between me and the officers. "This is my wife, Evelyn, and she has a confession to make."

Detective Murphy lowered his pistol and approached Evelyn helping her up to her feet. He looked at her face then at me and back at her again. "This doesn't make any sense. I saw her dead," he said confused.

My so called 'wife' paid off everyone to get me framed for her murder, to ruin my life and for her to disappear forever.

Evelyn looked at me again. I gave her the same look I gave her before in return— a huge over exaggerated smile. I dropped to my knees, put my hands behind my back and I waited for the officers to arrest me.

"Mr. and Mrs. Talbot, you're both under arrest for murder and conspiracy. Cuff them," Detective Murphy said while the officers charged at as.

I was pressed down to the ground on my stomach and watched Evelyn receive the same fate. I had run through the streets like a chicken without a head trying to hide, and to avoid being caught. I killed so many people— and for what? So I, in the end would kill the true person behind it all, which clearly I had been mistaken more than once. Then I would gladly turn myself in? Pretty funny when I thought about it. Everything has its way of working out in the end. We could be so focused on something or another and in a split second, with the change of an event, everything you believe or focus on will be changed.

We both sat on the curb of the street with two officers standing behind us. Detective Murphy was bringing someone over. Gregory was handcuffed and Detective Murphy sat him down next to me.

"Who's the lady?" Gregory asked, looking over at her. "A dazzling beauty if I may say so myself."

"Watch it Greg. That's my wife you're talking about," I answered sarcastically with a smile pressed on my face.

"Your wife? I thought she was murdered. Wasn't that the whole point of your spree?"

"I don't know who you are but please shut your mouth," Evelyn belted.

"Apparently I was fooled." I reached in close to Greg's ear and whispered, "I'm going to get you out of here. I just need you to tell Grace to just move on without me, for her to move far away from here like she always planned."

Gregory backed away slightly and pulled his lips into his mouth almost like he felt sorry for me. He waited a moment and then replied softly, "you got it."

A chariot pulled up and the detective opened the door and came to grab me by the arm.

"Watch your step," he said while he helped me up.

The other two officers brought Gregory and Evelyn over to the chariot and they too were helped by the detective.

One of the officers stepped up and sat beside Evelyn while Gregory and I sat beside each other just across from them. Detective Murphy closed the door and then jumped up to the front of the carriage. He said something to the driver which I couldn't hear and the carriage began to move.

Gregory looked at Evelyn and then at me. "I'm sorry to ask but is that your child?."

I knew why he was asking, clearly because he cared for Grace. "No. Just another bastard child who will never meet his father thanks to me," I said and grinned looking out the bar window.

Evelyn tried to pounce forward but was held back by the officer.

"Careful now," I mocked her never looking over to see her face. I honestly never wanted to look at her ever again.

"You're going to rot you son of a bitch," she hissed at me.

I looked over at her and answered simply, "in the same hole you are."

She looked at me with empty eyes and a pale face. I could tell she was not looking at me at that moment any longer. Her mind was being ravaged by a flood of reality that was hitting her. I looked at Gregory. He returned a glance and shrugged his shoulders. I smiled and then looked back out the window enjoying the fresh air against my face.

I could now see the police department but I was not nervous any longer. I had no fears, and had no reason to live. I just wanted to end all of this and I knew I would get hung for my crimes. I could have easily took my Colt pistol and blew mine and Evelyn's brains out, but I wanted everyone to see her for who she truly was. I knew the Bakers would be crushed at the death of their son by there bitch of a daughter but the truth sometimes hurts. Nonetheless, it was the truth after all and they deserved to know.

The carriage came to a complete stop and I could see a dozen cops running over to us. Detective Murphy opened the door and reached in pulling me outside. As the detective and I walked by the officers, I could hear them shuffling to grab the other two prisoners.

I looked over at The detective and said, "Can I just call you Owen?"

He looked at me with a raised eyebrow but then smiled "sure."

"Alright Owen, I have just one favor to ask you for all this?"

"Ok, I'm listening."

"Owen just let Gregory go. He shouldn't be involved in all this," I said.

"Phantom, don't tell me how to do my job," he said. He adjusted his top and guided me by the arm reaching in and opening the front door to the headquarters. I was guided through the office and stared at just like the time I was found at Tom Finagin's crime scene. I could see the door to the interrogation room I had been questioned in. I was sure Owen would open the door but he didn't. We kept walking down the hall to the last door straight ahead. The room was enormous and there was a beautifully varnished table made of the most solid wood anyone could get. A flag of our beautiful nation was standing proud at each side of the table and then there were two small tables laid out across the room with many chairs.

"Take a seat," the detective said to me. He released my arm and pointed with his entire hand towards the room.

I walked in and sat at the table on the left in the chair farthest from the monstrous table, which was on a podium of sorts. Owen closed the door and I looked around. I was all alone, then it hit me. I was going to have my trial.

CHAPTER 26: TRIAL

I waited only for a short time before the doors swung open. Grace ran towards me. She kissed me and hugged me as hard as she could.

"I know my dad will let you go," Grace said, completely lying to me, and too herself.

"There is no way out of this," I responded coldly not hugging her back.

"Yes, there is. Believe me."

"Grace, it was amazing and beautiful. It truly was but this is over now. We're over."

Grace looked at me. Her face puffed up instantly and tears streamed down her flushed cheeks. "This can't be over, Lawrence. This can't…"

"I turned myself in."

"I know you did, and I know your wife lied to you but I can talk to my dad."

"There is no way out of this. I need to die," I stated angrily.

"Stop saying that," Grace said through her sobbing. She smacked my chest. She hugged me and I leaned up against her as best as I could while my hands were tied behind my back.

"I love you Grace," I said.

She looked at me then wiped her eyes and replied softly, "And I love you."

I reached in and kissed Grace just as Evelyn was being escorted into the room. Evelyn looked over and spit at the ground in disgust.

Grace walked over and smacked Evelyn hard across the face hard. The officers who were escorting my beloved wife jumped at the impact but didn't dare say or do anything to the lead detective's daughter.

"You worthless bitch. How could you do that to him? He's such a good person?"

Evelyn licked her bloody lip and then looked up at Grace with a smile. "He 'was' a good person," she responded and then chuckled. The officers dragged her to a chair at the table adjacent to mine.

A handful of officials walked in, accompanied by a judge, many officers, and the son of a bitch, Commissioner of State. Everyone gathered around while the judge took his seat at the head table. Everyone began to take their seats also. Detective Murphy stood in the center of the room waiting for permission to begin.

Evelyn and I had our cuffs removed while we waited for the room to settle down. I waved Detective Murphy over. He reached in over the table revealing his pistol through the gaping hole of his shirt.

"What do you want?" he asked looking over at the judge, who was talking to a beautiful woman.

"I noticed Gregory never walked in."

"You turned yourself in so I decided to give you that one last request," he replied. He winked at me and took the center of the floor again.

I leaned back into my chair and exhaled deeply. Another innocent person wouldn't have their life ruined because of me.

"Permission to begin your honor?" Detective Murphy asked the judge.

"Permission granted," the judge said. He wiped his hands together and waved the beautiful woman away.

"The court is here tonight to judge the acts of Mr. Lawrence Talbot, also known as the Phantom Spree killer," he addressed. He pointed towards me and all eyes stared down at me.

He reached over and pointed at Evelyn next. "Also we're here to judge the acts of his wife, the apparently 'deceased,' Mrs. Evelyn Talbot."

Boos began to rain inside the courtroom. It was almost deafening.

"Order!" shouted the judge and the room slowly diminished its noise level until there wasn't a single peep.

"You may continue, Detective," the judge said pointing out to Owen.

"This woman, Mrs. Talbot, was apparently murdered last February by her husband, who sits across from her. He told me on multiple occasions that he was innocent and that clearly shows here if she's still alive. He turned to treachery in an act of revenge to murder the people who had taken his wife from him." The detective turned to me and walked over, leaning himself on my table. "Mr. Talbot, could you please start by confessing to exactly who you murdered since you turned yourself in?"

I cleared my throat and was about to speak when Owen waved his hand for me to rise to my feet. I nervously rose to my feet, screeching the chair across the floor, which echoed throughout the room. I cleared my throat again since the nerves had removed all the saliva from my throat.

I took a breath and then began. "New York, Detective, your honor," I said bowing to everyone. "I was misled into a road of evil which I am prepared to repay with my life. I killed thirteen people," I said. People began to talk amongst themselves.

A tomato came flying at me and hit me square in the eye. I jerked my head back since I wasn't expecting the blow.

"Order!" the judge shouted again, and slowly everyone silenced themselves. "Could you state for everyone who was killed and when?" The judge asked me.

"My first murder was of my landlord, Mr. Ben Johnson, who I attempted to bargain with to let me flee. I just wanted to change my clothing but he insisted on fighting me so I was forced to kill him. I killed three officers who were on duty, two were killed the same night Detective Murphy's partner, Annie Wilson, was killed in the catacombs of the cemetery."

"You killed Annie Wilson?" the judge asked, which didn't make sense since he knew the answer already. I'm sure he just wanted to hear his own voice.

"Yes, I blew her brains out. As I killed it, started to become easier and easier. I killed another officer just two nights ago during a chase while he was holding my brother-in-law captive."

"Where's your brother-in-law now?" Detective Murphy interrupted me asking.

"Evelyn murdered him just an hour ago," I responded. "Please let me continue." I cleared my throat again and proceeded with the kill count. " I killed a street thug and dumped his body by the ravine. The man I thought had killed my wife, named Vlad, and his two guards. I tortured them to death. I killed Conor Walsh, who my dear Wife escaped with, and finally three Irishmen yesterday in the battle between the Forty Thieves and The Bowery Boys."

The judge frowned his eyebrows and looked over at Evelyn. "Your statement," he ordered.

Evelyn didn't say a word. She just lowered her head down to the table.

"Speak now or forever be silenced," the judge shouted in a scary tone.

Evelyn knew she had no way out of this so she just remained quiet. Detective Murphy glanced at me. "Will you explain what happened?."

"Yes," I said simply.

Detective Murphy looked over at the judge, who nodded in agreement.

"Alright, begin."

I wanted this opportunity and it happened just as I had hoped. I pointed over at the commissioner, who instantly became flushed in the cheeks. He nervously looked around, awkwardly smiling.

"It all begins with Evelyn agreeing with the commissioner to have me fired. They would then split my severance pay, I on the other hand, believed I had received none since times were tough and he had no money to hand out. Evelyn planned with her brother, Joseph, to lead me to an apparent loan shark for money since she was sick. when actually she was pregnant with Conor Walsh's child while we were still living under the same roof."

People began shouting things at her and the officers had to hold people back. They shouted, "You whore", "slut", "night rider."

I waited a few moments until the noise level depleted and then I continued.

"In the end, the money I was lent was my actual severance pay that Evelyn had collected. She knew I would never be able to pay Vlad back so it would trigger the murder scene. First, she went with plan A which was to have me framed in the murder of the shop keeper, Tom Finagin."

Detective Murphy's eyes lit up. "Who killed Mr. Finagin?" he inquired.

"Her lover, my last kill, Conor Walsh. I would call him a mister but he is far from that."

"Stick to the story. Mr. Talbot," The judge said with a demanding voice.

I looked over at Evelyn before beginning because I wanted to see her face but she continued to look down at the table. Even from here I could tell the two-faced bitch was weeping herself dry.

"When plan A failed, they resorted to plan B which was for Evelyn to be murdered in front of me. Her brother dumped pig blood over her when I was hit over the head and severely dazed. 'My wife' and Conor ran away together, hoping never to return. But after getting to my brother-in-law, I was very persuasive and he agreed to aid me. When we approached Conor and my wife, she killed her own brother when his defenses were down. That is all." My body felt like a ton of bricks. I let myself go crashing onto the chair.

The judge looked at the detective and called him over. They spoke amongst each other as did everyone else in the room.

I looked over at the commissioner, who was drenched in sweat. He knew his time was up as two officers already stood near him just waiting for the call. Detective Murphy walked over to the commissioner's side but didn't say a word.

"Attention everyone," the judge called out. "Mrs. Talbot? How many months pregnant are you?"

Evelyn looked up slowly, trying to see the judge through her red puffy eyes. "Six months, your honor," she replied through her raspy voice.

The judge nodded and took a deep breathe. One could tell he was making his final decision. Then he handed out his sentence "I have decided that Mrs. Evelyn Talbot will be hung the day after her child birth."

People cheered frantically and the judge just raised his hand. "I'm not finished!" he shouted.

The room went silent.

"Mrs. Evelyn Talbot will be hung the day after her child birth, and I assure you Madame that your child will go to the greatest orphanage in the State."

Evelyn cried but I could see the look of relief in her face.

"The commissioner is now stripped of his rank and will also be hung on the same day."

The commissioner attempted to rise from his chair to flee but was shoved down by the detective and surrounding officers.

The judge looked over at me with a dark glance until his face muscles relaxed. "For turning yourself and your wife in, and being very helpful to the case, I have decided you will be hung the same day as the other two and not a minute sooner."

Everyone in the room again cheered. Oddly enough, I joined in on their excitement. All this bullshit would finally come to an end.

"Mr. Gregory Timmons, who has been tried earlier today, has been sentenced with the same time in prison. But when the three are to be hung, Mr. Timmons will be released. That is all," the judge said. He got up from his chair and exited the room.

I looked over at the detective, who clearly lied to me but he did not return my stare. He was busy handing the ex-commissioner off to a few officers. Evelyn too was being taken out. I just sat comfortably in my chair waiting to be taken out also.

When Detective Murphy was done handing off the other two criminals, he approached me. "Come now. I'm going to take you to your cell."

I offered no resistance and rose to my feet. He walked me out of the room. I honestly was glad to get out of there. Far too many people in my space was making me nervous, or maybe it was the speaking in front of a crowd.

The detective took me along a dark corridor with only a few barely lit candles and opened a cell releasing the cuffs and guiding me in. I walked in and the detective closed the cell door instantly. I heard a shuffle and looked back to the dark corner, where Gregory was resting against a wall.

I sat beside him and I let my body drop hard, just as I did in the courtroom. I looked at him. He returned the stare and we both nodded.

Some time passed and we could here footsteps coming from down the hall. The barely lit cell didn't help us see who was entering as the front gate opened. I got to my feet and stepped forward to see the ex-Commissioner walking in. I smiled and he frowned. That's just how I expected the next three months to be between us.

CHAPTER 27: THE WITCH

The cell floor was very cold but I couldn't complain. I was going to be put out of my misery very soon; there were approximately two and a half months remaining now. My beard was thicker now, then again so was Greg's and the ex-Commissioner's. The 'ex', I'm just going to call him, had a couple of bruises on his face—thanks to me of course for assisting in fucking me over.

I kept waiting for the moment Evelyn would be put in the cage with us but I guess being a female she would be separated from the males to avoid rape. I wouldn't touch her anyway but I couldn't speak for the other two. Men being trapped and alone for a long time can change the way a man thinks. Couldn't blame them I guess. She is attractive and they're lonely. Either way, if she hadn't come in the two weeks since we had been locked up, then there was no way she was coming now.

I crouched up from a lying position to see the morning sun beaming through the window. The light reflected on the ground revealing someone in the shadows. I could see the figure standing there. Without getting closer, it was impossible to determine just who was there. Had someone been brought here while I was sleeping? That wouldn't be a surprise since I was pretty knocked out. I had probably gotten only a couple of hours of sleep each night since I was incarcerated here. Someone could have blown the building up and I would have slept through it.

"Hello, who's there?" I asked pressing my body forward and squinting my eyes to adjust to the shape.

"I am whoever you want me to be," replied the mysterious but familiar voice.

I contemplated since I had the voice's identity on the tip of my tongue but it just wouldn't come to me.

The figure emerged revealing herself from the shadows; it was the voodoo lady that fixed my arm.

"What the hell are you doing here?" I asked in confusion.

She smiled at me. The darkness embraced her dark skin but her white teeth shone ever brightly.

"I'm here to help you just like the last time."

"What can you do for me now? I don't need saving," I said wholeheartedly.

"The only way you could die peacefully is if you kill the ex," she stated and pointed over at the sleeping man.

How did she know I was calling him 'the ex' if I had never mentioned him to her in our previous conversation. "I will not kill anymore," I proclaimed.

She approached me and grabbed a hex bag from her pocket. She shoved the hex bag down my throat, making me nearly choke to death. She released me and I gasped for air. The hex bag was the size of a fist. How the hell did I swallow it whole?

"Now kill him. Kill the final person who wronged you," her enchanting voice commanded. I wanted to object to her order but my body began to practically move on it' own. It was the witch's black magic again. I knelt down over the commissioner and grabbed him by his top. He opened his eyes startled, awoken from his sleep. I head butted him over and over again until he was dead. The blood trickled down my face. I wasn't sure if it was mine or his but Mr. Ex was dead and the witch was right.

"Thank you," I said looking back at her. The witch had disappeared. "Hello? Where did you go?"

I could see the figure in the darkness again. I got up and wiped the blood off my face with my shirt. "I was thanking you." As I uttered the words, it wasn't the witch who came from the darkness it was Greg. His face was frightened at the gruesome scene.

"What the fuck did you do?" Greg shouted. He ran to 'the Ex' to see if he was alive. We both knew that was impossible at this point.

"The witch from the church told me to do it. Well she practically forced me. She made me ingest a hex bag like last time."

Gregory looked at me confused. "What witch? Hex bag? I don't follow."

"Remember when we left the church after speaking to Father Edwards that night and the witch approached us and fixed my arm?" I asked trying to make him remember.

Gregory pointed at my arm. "Your arm is fixed?" he asked rhetorically.

"What the fuck's gotten into you. Of course it's fixed!" I belted, now annoyed. I looked down at my arm and noticed it was paralyzed.

Gregory approached me and told me to sit. I did so still looking at my arm in confusion. "Lawrence, you're scaring me, man. Your arm was never fixed, and we never left the church that night. We slept there since Father Edwards gave us shelter."

My head spun in circles. I had imagined all that, I was crazy and it didn't make sense. My mind made it seem so real. "Wait a minute. I paid her the money Father Edwards gave me," I insisted now certain there was a misunderstanding.

Gregory sat in front of me and took a big gulp as he spoke. "You went outside for a moment and I saw you toss the money down the sewer hatch. I never mentioned it because I thought you were storing it for escape money and had decided to just fight your way to free Grace. It wasn't my place to ask so I ignored it."

I thought that was all but then Gregory began to speak again. "There's one more thing. When you dropped the money into the sewer hatch I saw you take out your blade and cut the surgery wound I had performed. I'm assuming that's where the hex bag went?" he asked rhetorically since he already knew the answer.

"Yes," I muttered completely ashamed.

Gregory got up to his feet and walked over to the cage. "Guards, help there has been a murder."

"What are you doing? Clearly I was crazy. I'm sorry," I tried to explain.

"I know, Lawrence. I'm doing this for your own protection."

The guards rushed the cell and laid Gregory and I down on the ground until I admitted what I had done. I was a delusional fuck up of a man. This was just the cherry I needed on top of this cake to not feel any remorse for myself when I hung to death. I was dangerous and needed to be stopped.

The guards shackled me to the wall where I would remain for the rest of my sentence. Gregory was free to move around, which he did. The stink of the Ex's blood was foul for a few weeks but it eventually faded away like his memory. Gregory and I never spoke again after that day which was over a month ago. If I calculated correctly, there were approximately two weeks until my death sentence.

CHAPTER 28: UNFAMILIAR SOUND

A handful of guards stormed into the cell, and unshackled me and dragged me away. Gregory watched on. I could see no expression on his face. The day of being friends was clearly long gone as he most likely feared me.

"Where are you taking me?" I asked struggling to find my voice.

"Any day now you're dying so there are some people that want to see you," one of the guards explained. They brought me into the interrogation room I had sat in half a year ago.

I looked over at a mirror wall the room had and could see my awful appearance. My beard was long and shaggy, and my hair was oiled to shit, all curly and messy. Anyone could tell I hadn't bathed in months. The hair wouldn't be the clue to that. It would be the smell off shit reeking off of my body. I actually felt sorry for whomever was coming in.

The door opened and Detective Murphy walked in, accompanied by Mr. and Mrs. Baker. I couldn't believe the sight and bowed my head down ashamed. Detective Murphy walked over to me and uncuffed my hands. I looked up shocked not expecting that to happened ever again.

"The Bakers trust you and have requested you're unshackled for them to speak to you."

I didn't say anything to him and I just looked over at John and Susan while they sat across from me at the table. I ran my hands through my hair hoping to at least control some of the mess. I pressed my palms from my forehead to the back of my neck a few times.

"God have mercy on your soul," Susan said nodding to me.

"Do not have pity on me. I am a demon and deserve everything I'm going to experience."

John edged forward leaning half of his body on the table. "No, you are our only real child. Though you weren't born from us, you were the only one to always be yourself." Susan cried into John's shoulder as he finished speaking. He grabbed his wife and they both sobbed.

"I'm sorry you two had to experience what you did."

"Please don't apologize. There's no need. We completely understand why you lost your mind. I believe I probably would have done the same," John assured me.

Even though I was sure of what was going to happen to me and I wanted it to happen, I felt some relief knowing that I wasn't the only person that would fight the entire world in the name of love or revenge. Whatever you call it, they are intertwined when someone takes your soul mate from you.

I smiled at the Bakers, which was the first smile I had given since the courtroom nearly three months ago.

"We came here simply to tell you that we love you and we will be there for you tomorrow praying that your soul goes to heaven," Susan said She put her hand on mine.

I smiled. " Thank you so much for everything," I responded and the tears came to my eyes. I didn't wipe them. I wanted the Bakers to see my tears, which were real tears— tears of joy. They stood up and approached the door. John knocked on it a few times. The detective opened the door and the Baker's left the room. I looked down at my hands and let go an enormous exhale of air. It was a relief to know some people knew why I did what I did.

The door opened again and Grace walked in, smiling as she came to kiss me. I stuck my hand out towards her. I was still seated with my head facing forward.

"Sit," I ordered and she did.

"Why can't I kiss you?" she asked grabbing my hand.

"Why haven't you left yet?" I asked ignoring her question and asking my own in return.

"I wanted to see you one last time before going."

"So you won't see me die?" I asked rhetorically. I was actually glad she wasn't.

"No, I'm leaving tonight. I'm heading out to California on a three month boat ride down through South America."

"I'm glad. You should have just left without doing this to yourself. Now this is what you're going to remember every time you close your eyes and see me. Well, until you find my replacement," I said. I pointed at my face and swung circles around my head in the air showing emphasis on my appearance.

"How could you say that? I don't want a replacement. I want..."

"Just stop Grace, seriously," I said cutting her off.

"How could you treat me like this after what we had together."

"What did we have? One night of amazing sex, and a similar friend we could confide in." I knew that was harsh but I wanted her to leave. It was paining me to see her and not be able to escape with her. A little bit of me really regretted turning myself in and wished I had just run away with Grace and raised a family on the other side of the country. I couldn't tell her what I felt. It would make everything more difficult for her to leave. I just wanted her to move on with her life.

I wanted to be erased from history so nobody would ever know I existed.

Grace bawled, completely upset. She got up from her chair and smacked me in the face. "You disgusting pig!" she shouted and stormed out of the room.

I began to cry. I knew it was for the best but my heart yearned to just run after her and make love to her. I really wanted it but I knew it was far too late. Even if I managed to escape now she would never take me back after I spoke those words.

Detective Murphy charged into the room. Nearly slicing my wrists, he cuffed me again then grabbed my arm and took me to my cell.

"I can't believe she even cared for you. Just pitiful."

"She is a wonderful person you should be proud of," I replied.

"Don't you ever talk about my daughter again. You hear me?" I could see a fire in Detective Murphy's eyes that I had only seen once before— the day of the Five Points Massacre. He opened the cell and shackled me to the wall.

The night came and I began to hear a commotion down the hall. I squinted my eyes trying to adjust to the light that was turned on.

"Gregory, you hear that?" I asked my old friend.

"I'm not deaf," he muttered still lying on the ground facing the other way.

I crunched my nose and made a face to the back of Greg's head. I could clearly hear a woman screaming and it hit me—Evelyn was having the baby. The screams went on for at least a dozen hours and then the halls filled with an unfamiliar sound, the sound of a baby crying.

I smiled and looked out into the night sky and stared at the moon since it was the last time I would ever see it's beauty.

CHAPTER 29: DEBT'S PAID

I stood at the window looking up at the cloudy sky. I took in many deep breathes enjoying fresh air for a few more moments. I could hear a vast amount of people talking outside. There was a huge gathering happening. The only way a gathering this enormous happened was when there was a hanging being presented. Many criminals were beheaded in the back of the department, so when there was a hanging everyone would come out for the show. Hanging was the only public execution they would display because it wasn't very gruesome for children to watch.

The door at the end of the hallway opened and I could hear a flurry of footsteps approaching the cell. I didn't look over to see who was coming to get me, I kept my gaze out the window at the cloudy sky that blocked the sun's warm embrace. I was sad because I had the chance to see the moon one last time and I really was hoping to see the sun with a blue sky. I guess it was a day of mourning for those who would see justice delivered. God would rain the tears of the many through the clouds to reflect his children's pain.

The cell door opened and I finally looked over since there wasn't anything to look at out to the sky. The officers approached Gregory and helped him to his feet. "Congratulations, you're a free man," and officer said helping Gregory out of the cell. Gregory started to walk out and then turned looking at me between two of the cell bars. He nodded at me, and I nodded back and that was the last time I would ever see my friend again.

The officers approached me next and unshackled me, helping me to my feet. They stepped aside and Detective Murphy walked through accompanied by a priest. A thin man with boney fingers.

"This is the new priest to replace the late Father Edwards. His name is Father Stevens and he will be praying for you and Evelyn at the hanging."

I smiled at the priest and then looked down to the ground.

"Is there anything you would like to confess or tell God before we go outside?" Father Stevens asked me.

"Yes. Tell God not to pity me, and give me the judgement I deserve," I said as I spit to the ground.

Father Stevens stiffened up his upper lip and turned walking away. I smiled and was dragged out to the hallway where I stood behind Evelyn. We were both cuffed behind our backs and stood there waiting for the time to arrive. The doors were closed but I could hear the chanting of many folks coming from the outside. If I didn't know it was my own death, I would think there was a fucking parade happening just outside.

The doors opened and we were escorted through the crowds. People screamed and cursed at me and Evelyn while we walked through the crowds. The officers held people back but punches would sneak by. I would just grimace to the sudden pain but kept walking. The officers did the best they could but my face and body were definitely hurting now. A rock flew through the air and cracked Evelyn in the forehead. She cried out and turned her face over to me hiding from the direction of the stone in case more followed. I could see a huge gash opening across her forehead as the blood streamed down.

"You ok?" I asked honestly not knowing why.

Evelyn looked at me with the puppy face she used to make that made my heart melt and kiss her. "Yes, I'm fine," she replied coldly and then was guided to the stage.

We stood at the foot of the steps leading up to the stage. I looked up and noticed two nooses.

I remembered 'the Ex' and how he could have been here with us right now if I hadn't killed him. Maybe he would have been the one to catch the stone inside of Evelyn.

The detective and Father Stevens walked up the steps and were met by two men, who were already present on the stage. I'm sure one of those fuckers would be the one to pull on the lever to send me to my impending doom. I almost envied them, the world's greatest job being able to kill people and get away with it.

The officers walked us up the steps and we were placed facing the crowd. The nooses were right behind us and the lever pullers were next to us but off to the side.

The detective walked forward and raised his hands, motioning for the crowd to silence. There had to be at least two thousand people present for the execution.

"Now Father Stevens, who is the new priest of our parish, will pray for the damned souls."

Father Stevens stepped forward and began doing the sign of the cross. I wanted to do the sign also but my hands were tied behind my back. He then began, "Our Father who art in heaven..."

The world suddenly feel silent as I was in a void of nothingness. "Thy will be done, on earth as it is in heaven , Give us th..."

I really felt empty inside. But my heart raced quickly as I could not hear a single word the priest was saying again. After a few moments I could hear again. "glory for ever and ever. Amen."

Everyone replied in a humble tone, "Amen."

I looked down at the crowd and could see the Johnson family weeping in the front row. I really did regret killing Ben but the fool left me no choice. I could see Grace, which sent me into a flurry of confusion. I also saw the voodoo lady again standing randomly in the crowd. I closed my eyes tightly and shook my head. I then opened one eye slowly to see if she was there—she was not. I had made her disappear thankfully. I looked over to the right. I saw a person approaching and the voodoo lady jumped up in my face which made me jump to the left and I screamed like a little girl. The entire crowd went silent and then belted out in a cheer of laughter and jokes. I could make out a few words such as, "he's crazy", "he's lost his mind."

I settled down and stood there again waiting. Father Stevens stepped down the steps and joined the crowd looking up at me and Evelyn, holding his bible with both hands across his stomach.

Detective Murphy then began stating our crimes and I knew I had no more than two minutes to live. I closed my eyes and began to breathe deeply. My nerves started to rush forward.

"These two criminals are to be hung in view of the public for their heinous actions against the State of New York. Evelyn Talbot, to my left, for conspiracy of murder, murder of the first degree, and Treason to the State for fraud on her life. To my right, Lawrence Talbot, for fourteen counts of murder by the first degree, and evading his capture for over four months. The State of New York sentences both of you to die." As the detective uttered those words, thunderous shakes came from the earth and from up above, rain drops began to fall. This was quickly followed by a heavy rainstorm. Most people stayed and watched. The nooses were placed around our necks. I looked over at Evelyn and she looked at me.

"I'm sorry," Evelyn said, which caught me by surprise.

"Me too," I responded. A bag was put over my face. I began to breathe heavily. I looked forward and could barely distinguish what was rain and what was actually people. I could hear Evelyn crying aloud. We waited for the moment where the floor would collapse beneath us.

"Evelyn, it's alright. Embrace it!" I shouted but she didn't respond. She just continued crying. I knew that nobody could see me so I smiled as wide as I could and closed my eyes looking up to the sky, feeling the rain pressing the bag closer to my face.

I muttered my final words. "It's finally over."

In a split second, the ground collapsed beneath me and I could feel the absolute guillotine choke of the noose against my neck. I couldn't think of anything at that moment just on the pain that I was experiencing. I couldn't breathe and my neck felt off. I figured my windpipe had been broken. I regretted ever letting this happen to me but before I could do anything, I felt myself slipping away. The cheers became faint and then everything went black. The cheers, the hate, and the pain was all over.

CHAPTER 30: NEW YORK 1899

Fifteen years had passed since the death of the most lethal serial killer America had ever endured to date. Many people didn't even remember Lawrence's existence, but there was always a few that would. Eventually, Lawrence would get his wish and people would forget his name, making him lost in history.

A home in New Jersey housed John and Susan Baker, and their fifteen year old grandson, who was named Alexander Baker. The bastard son of Conor Walsh. Alexander was a troubled boy because he was often teased and harassed because of his mother's past.

Susan grabbed Alexander from school one afternoon as he approached her upset.

"What happened this time, Alex" Susan asked while she wrapped her arms around him embracing him completely.

Alex looked up with soulless eyes and responded. "Frank called my mother a whore again."

"I know it's hard but you must ignore that. People will always grab our weaknesses and use it against us. Besides how could he really know if she was one. It's not like he was there too see it right?" Susan asked and then helped him to their car.

Alexander didn't say a word. He just waited for his grandmother to open the door so he could step inside. The Bakers were one of the few people to own a car. Since the Bakers had suffered dearly, people had decided to band together and donate to help the family start a new life.

That night, Susan made dinner and called out to Alexander from the kitchen window towards the barn. John got comfortable and helped himself to a serving of her famous soup.

"The boy just won't come," Susan said worried, still looking out the window.

"When his stomach grumbles he will come, don't worry," John said slurping a spoonful.

Susan joined John at the table and began to serve herself when she heard the back door open. John and Susan both looked to see Alexander walk inside, extremely distraught. His eyes carried murderous intent in them. John looked down to see Alexander holding a gun. It wasn't not just any gun. It was the famous gun of the Phantom Spree Killer— the Colt.

"You fucking lied to me," Alexander belted, pointing the gun towards his grandparents. John got up quickly, As his chair fell over, he sprang to the side of the table with his hands pressed forward motioning for Alexander to calm down..

"Alexander, stop this. Give me the gun," John said. He walked slightly forward moving around the table.

"Don't you fucking move. You just forgot to mention who my real father was. Did you know I stay up at night imagining myself murdering everyone around me? It's a proven fact that being a murderer can be hereditary."

John looked over at Susan and she returned the shallow stare. They both knew what he was insinuating and it looked like he might be right. If studies were correct, then Alexander was actually Lawrence's son.

"You lied to me and I can't resist any longer," Alexander said. He pressed the trigger—BAM! BAM!. Two shots to John's chest sent him sprawling over the dinner table, sending everything crashing to the ground. Susan ran to grab her husband, who died instantly in her arms. Susan looked up to see Alexander standing above her, pointing the barrel of the gun just inches away from her face. She wept at her husband's death but also wept knowing it was impossible for her to make it out of this alive.

The Colt had a similar kill many years ago on now retired, Detective Murphy's, assistant Annie Wilson. History would repeat itself again.

"No, Alex don't do this!" Susan shouted.

BAM!

Alexander stood above his dead grandparents covered in their blood. He held the smoking Colt at his side. He stared smiling and looked over at the other side of the kitchen. The voodoo witch returned a smile to him with her very white teeth.

ONE LAST THING....

If you enjoyed this book I'd be very grateful if you'd post a short review on Amazon. Your support really does make a difference and I read all the reviews personally so I can get your feedback and make my future books even better.

Thanks again for your support!

Made in the USA
Charleston, SC
25 November 2015